ROBERT

WALKER

Corey Mesler

Livingston Press
The University of West Alabama

ISBN 13: 978-1-60489-172-0, trade paper

Library of Congress Control Number 2016944230

Typesetting and page layout: Amanda Nolin, Joe Taylor
Proofreading: Teresa Boykin, Joe Taylor, Amanda Nolin, Tricia Taylor,
Mary Slimp
Cover design: Amanda Nolin

Cover photo: David Tankersley
Author photo: Sandra Smith-McDougall

For Cheryl, Toby and Chloe, always
and for Peter Coyote

This is a work of fiction:
any resemblance
to persons living or dead is coincidental.

Livingston Press is part of The University of West Alabama,
and thereby has non-profit status.
Donations are tax-deductible:
brothers and sisters, we need 'em.

ROBERT WALKER

Corey Mesler

"There are no odds to beat, no rules to set a limit on bad luck, and at each moment we begin again, as ripe for a low blow as we were the moment before."
—Paul Auster

"Apaches in the alleys keep us walking the street."
—Elliot Baker

"I haven't got any special religion this morning. My God is the God of Walkers. If you walk hard enough, you probably don't need any other god."
—Bruce Chatwin

"In the Judeo-Christian tradition man is seen in the first place as a pilgrim, in transit, in a predicament, in a fix, fallen.
—Walker Percy

"Giant of a man, /homeless/in autumn wind."
—Issa

PART ONE

1

Memphis, Tennessee, Monday, October 2, 2006

It was on the two hundred and twenty-fifth day of his abandonment that Robert Walker awoke in his cardboard box with half his face immobilized. Right eye droopy, with no blink power. Corner of mouth turned downward in half-frown. Ear sore yet numb. Temple tender, jawline painful. He shook his head as if perhaps he just needed to rattle the contents and the picture would right itself.

A picture. That's what he needed, a mirror, a self portrait. A portrait of the self. He needed to look at his face to see what had happened. He felt as if he'd been to the dentist and the Novocain had affected one side of his head. Perhaps he dreamed he was at the dentist. Perhaps Dream Novocain had altered his appearance.

There was no one to contact, no house to visit for a mirror, or anything else. Robert Walker was alone this morning. There used to be Lyn. Lyn was a spook, a ghost now. Robert could not think about her. Lyn had become too dear to him, that's the truth. Better that she forgets him. By now she would have forgotten him. It had been two hundred and twenty-five days.

2

ROBERT Walker exited his box and stretched his limbs. The morning was nippy and the dew was bright and cool, wee contact lenses on green weed stalks, among the dying grasses. Robert's box, his cardboard pallet, sat at the edge of what in Memphis was called The Old Forest. At one end of The Old Forest sat a park, Overton Park, and a zoo. At the other the end the endless project of Interstate 40 and Sam Cooper Boulevard. It was a portion of the transcontinental road that broke down into unremitting construction as if it were always in the process of being born. Robert was on the interstate side of the park, just off a playground, secreted near some large oaks. His box practically blended in with the dirt brown leaves and tree trunks and rot. He felt safe in this place.

The park was quiet. There was another camper sleeping on a bench in the gazebo. Robert thought it was Whiskey Dave. Rosy-fingered dawn was about to crack her knuckles and let it all begin. The air smelled slightly of urine.

Now a bathroom was needed. In the bathroom there would be a mirror. Robert had used up many of the service station bathrooms in the area. More than once he had been told the restrooms were for customers only. He had to travel further and further from his box to find a place to shit and pee and wash up.

This morning he went east on Summer Avenue. He knew he looked like a bum. He knew the passing motorists looked at him as if he were detritus, a form of rot. Societal rot. The clothes he wore had started to show tatters and loose threads and some odd stains that Robert didn't remember garnering. His jacket especially looked seedy and fetid. One morning a carload of teenagers had thrown a soft drink cup at him, laughing off into the distance as he stood there with glairy drink on his face. The same face that was now half-paralyzed.

Robert hiked past Family Dollar, Gate City Hardware, an antique warehouse, a Bargain Depot. And the deathless Paris Adult Theater where one could see triple-x films almost any time of day. Excepting this early it was closed and quiet. A film was advertised but Robert could not make out the title in the shadows of the entrance. Something that looked like Double Peptide.

About a half-mile down Summer Avenue Robert found a Shell station that he had never used. The men's bathroom was not locked. Things were looking up. The doorknob was coated with transudate.

Robert stood before the greyish mirror and took stock of his ravaged appearance. One side of his face hung loose as if it were the skin of a shar-pei. There was an odd downward turn to his mouth, half hidden by his grimy beard. And his eye was almost half-closed except that he couldn't close it. He could close it with his finger.

And his ear hurt like hell.

What new curse is this? Robert Walker asked of the world.

He took care of his bodily needs, washed as well as he could at the sink, getting soapy water in his eye because it did not close when he splashed his face. Ow, damn, Robert Walker said.

He took a damp paper towel and wiped down his clothes.

Before leaving he took another look in the mirror. It certainly was an odd visage that stared back at him. An old man, a man spent. He didn't recognize himself.

Who is that dirty half-wit? Robert Walker thought.

He set out then to try and scrounge some breakfast. While walking further east on Summer Avenue it occurred to him that he probably had had a stroke. Would he be able to think this clearly if he had had a stroke? He didn't know.

Robert crossed the viaduct over Industrial Park and Owen Lumber. There was a Title Max, a JC's Quick Cash, Leahy's cabins. When he was small he wanted his father and mother to take him to Leahy's for a night out. The place looked like something out of some dim 50s film noir, a place Alan Ladd and Veronica Lake might hole up. He tried to explain this to his parents, why he wanted just one night at Leahy's cabins. It never happened.

The sidewalks were mostly free of other pedestrians. Yet, even this early there was a guy on the sidewalk with a hot tamale cart. Tamales for breakfast on a bleak urban street in Memphis, Tennessee.

Robert found a Walgreens he could stand in front of and cadge some change. Walgreens would run him off quickly enough but, sometimes, not before he got enough money for breakfast. He thought maybe this new affliction, this half-face, would make it more difficult to bum money. Or maybe it would make it easier, like those guys he'd seen faking leg problems to gain sympathy from passersby.

Robert Walker

"Thp—pare thom change?" he asked the first person to pass him, a middle aged woman wearing a neck brace.

She turned away and hustled into Walgreens.

Robert was finding speech difficult. This is indeed odd, he thought.

After standing there for about 15 minutes, greeting everyone who passed, Robert had enough money for some coffee and a sausage and biscuit. He headed for McDonald's.

Most McDonald's hated to see him coming. But he also noticed many other street people eating at McDonald's.

"Thauthage b—p—bithkit," Robert Walker said to the pimply faced teen at the register.

"Huh?" he said back.

Robert tried again.

"Breakfast biscuit?" the teen asked.

"Yepth," Robert Walker said. "And coffee."

When he had gotten his food he sat near the window to enjoy the sunny warmth there and relish his hot meal. The early morning light was as gentle as a benediction. Robert almost forgot that he only had half a face.

3

BINDLESTIFF.

The word appeared on the screen inside Robert Walker's head. He had a vague idea what it meant. Bum.

Robert Walker was a bindlestiff, a bum. He had taken up an itinerant lifestyle.

Lifestyle. That was a word he was eschewing. He was leaving it behind like so much else.

Robert Walker was on the bum with a face half-paralyzed.

He stared out onto Summer Avenue, surely one of the more depressing displays that modern man had concocted. An avenue of poor commerce and rundown businesses, a dead-end on civilization's inexorable parade. Further on prostitutes brazenly walked the sidewalks, women in plastic skirts, brief as desk drawers, even in the daytime. Further on there were pay by the hour motels, cheap car lots, dodgy nightclubs. The butt-end of progress. Robert Walker, though, was not depressed by his vista. Not this morning.

The sun felt good on his face, his crippled face.

The coffee was passable, hot at least. He was having a hard time drinking, dribbling into his beard like a child. Should he get a straw? That would look fairly ridiculous. The biscuit tasted vaguely of sawdust and chemicals and spicy meat. It was a fine breakfast.

Robert Walker looked around the pre-fab dining area of the McDonald's. A young couple with that freshly scrubbed, freshly sexed-up aura about them. A man and his son. Another vagrant, eating his breakfast burrito as if it were cheese and he a starving rat.

And a young, attractive woman who was openly staring at him.

Robert Walker could not look away. She was beautiful. Blond and tanned and wearing her good health as if it were a cloak. She gave Robert a half-smile. He could only half-smile back.

"Sorry," she said.

"What?" Robert responded.

"Sorry to stare."

"Oh," Robert said.

"Sorry about the bell's palsy, too. I've been there."

What was she talking about? Robert must have looked quizzical.

"You do know it's bell's palsy, right? Making half your face fall apart?"

"No," Robert said. "Wuzzit again?"

"Bell's. Palsy."

"Uh."

"Comes on suddenly, reasonless. Stays a while. Goes away just as mysteriously. Like love."

Here the beautiful woman laughed.

Robert tried to laugh in return. It came out like a huff and a puff.

Now she stood and moved toward him. She looked like an actress Robert liked a lot. He couldn't think of her name.

"May I?" she said, indicating another chair at Robert's table.

"Hffn," Robert said.

"Gayla Calley," she said, sitting down. She held out

a hand.

Robert took the hand.

"Gwyneth Paltrow," Robert said.

Gayla Calley cocked her head like a dog and laughed a short laugh again.

"That is not your name," she said.

"Sthorry," Robert Walker said. "I jutht figured out who you look like."

"Gwyneth Paltrow? Gosh damn. Thanks. Haven't heard that before."

Robert Walker started to say something else. Something clever, something to keep this beautiful woman at his table. He had nothing.

Robert Walker sat silently staring into Gayla Calley's blue eyes.

"Did you see a doctor about the palsy?" she now asked.

"Jutht thith morning," Robert said.

"You saw a doctor this morning?"

"Jutht...thith..."

"You only contracted it this morning?"

Robert nodded.

"Well, seeing a doctor is optional. There's really nothing they can do with it. They might give you some cortisone, which, truthfully, you don't want. They may give you antibiotics, but, again, you probably don't want that. Oh, sorry. Reason I know all this is that I had bell's palsy. About 3 years ago when I was just starting graduate school."

"Huh," Robert Walker said. "It went away."

"Yes. Poof. Just like that."

"Huh."

"It's idiopathic."

"Hm."

"Anyway. Wait. What's your name? You have mine."

"Robert Walker," Robert Walker said.

"It's nice to meet you, Robert Walker," Gayla Calley said. "I didn't mean to intrude. It's just that it's such a strange, otherworldly malady, I thought you might need some commiseration, some reassurance that it is only temporary."

"I did. I do," Robert said.

"Well, then, my work here is through."

Robert panicked. His one good eye went wide. His mouth contorted. He sensed a globlet of spittle on the dead side of his lips. Gayla sat up straight, surprised by this paroxysm.

"You ok?" she asked.

"What are you?" Robert spat out, as well as he could spit, which was not well at all.

Gayla laughed. "A peri?" she said.

Robert Walker was confused. Perry who, he wondered.

"Do you mean what do I do for a living?" Gayla said, with a lightsome smile. "I teach. English teacher at the U of M."

"Ah," Robert said.

"Where I have to go now."

Robert's heart sank. But, really, what did he expect they would do together? Gayla recognized disappointment on his features.

"Would you want to meet later? Lunch? Can you meet me on campus, at the student center around noon? We could have a good talk."

"Yeth," Robert said.

Gayla stood and stuck out her hand again. Robert took her slim, soft offering in his still grimy paw. He could not take his eyes—eye—off her face. She was really so lovely.

"See you then, Robert Walker," Gayla said.

"Ok," Robert Walker said.

4

ROBERT Walker sat for another fifteen minutes at his table, studying the sunshine scattering off windshields and shop windows. The bum, the other bum, was singing something which sounded vaguely like "Rocky Raccoon." Robert did not even turn to look at him, though he felt his approach.

"What's up, Doctor?" He was standing so close to Robert that Robert could feel something brush against his sleeve.

Robert looked up at him. He recognized him from the Mission. Robert thought his name was Willy. Willy was a black man in his 60s with skin the color of a wet teabag, and his face was ripe with white whiskers, stuck in at random, like pins in a pincushion. At the mission Willy was avoided, left to himself for the most part, because he didn't talk much sense. Even among the homeless Willy was an outcast.

"Hey," Robert said.

"What's up, Cap'n?" Willy said.

Robert looked him in the eye. He held his stare for an uncomfortable few seconds and finally Robert turned away, fixing his gaze once again on the brightly lit panorama of Summer Avenue.

"Coffee," Willy said.

"Biscuit," Willy said.

"Say, Corporal," Willy said. "Your face is melting."

Robert turned back toward Willy. In the background there was a confab going on behind the counter. Three employees were huddling, making plans, Robert figured, on how to get the gutterpups out of their establishment. Robert was lumped in with Willy. It was just as well.

"Better go," Robert said.

"Say, Ensign," Willy said. "Your face is melting."

"Yeth," Robert said.

"Say, Cap'n," Willy said. "You like bush?"

Robert stood up, nearly knocking Willy off his wobbly pins. He pushed past him. The McDonald's employees were emerging from behind the counter, led by a tall white man in short-sleeved shirt and tie, apparently their leader. Robert hustled past them.

Once outside Robert Walker looked back. The posse was surrounding Willy. Robert almost felt sorry for the moonstruck Willy. Robert imagined that Willy was explaining himself to the group, an explanation Robert would have liked to hear.

5

ROBERT stood on the sidewalk on Summer Avenue and looked long both ways as if the homely street represented two paths diverged in a yellow wood. He could walk east, moving toward the unknown, toward the hookers and daytime motels. It was a part of Memphis where he had not spent much time. Hookers made him nervous. They were not above picking on the homeless, with whom they were occasionally condescending and occasionally maternal.

Or he could travel west back toward Midtown where he was more comfortable. Midtown was a great place to sponge handouts. Robert had to get some money before lunch and he had to pass the hours till then. And, if he could, he had to make himself more presentable. Even on his best days he could not tell if he smelled bad. Today, he had only half his olfactory glands working.

While walking back westward from whence he had come Robert Walker's right eye began to sting. He rubbed it with a knuckle. That made it worse. Every bit of road dust and urban grit lodged there. He also became aware of the bright red pain beginning to radiate from his ear like a stain. He made it back to the park on the edge of the Old Forest. The gazebo was now empty and he didn't see Whiskey Dave anywhere. Robert thought about Dave. Without him Robert wouldn't have even a modicum of street savvy, wouldn't be able to rough it as much as he could. Dave was a sort of King of the Road, in the old sense of the term. Robert picked one of the benches in the gazebo and lay down on it. He put his hands under his head the way he used to when a child, when he used to lie in bed, sleep far away, and watch the lights from the cars going down his street move across the ceiling of his bedroom, spectral and stately. It was comforting. Outside the world was active, noisy, alive, and here he was inside, in his secure bed, under freshly laundered sheets, and under the time-honored aegis of his benevolent parents.

Robert's idea was that Dave had seen much, had traveled and hoboed and suffered both inner and outer malefactions, but had always kept Memphis a part of him. And, for Robert, a big part of Memphis, now, in these latter days, was Dave.

Robert did not close his eyes. He saw the world atilt. The playground area, with its red and forest green roofed slide and swings and jungle gym, was also deserted.

Now he lay and watched the early morning traffic on East Parkway, further south a divided street of opulent homes, tony upscale modern next to older manses. Every car seemed to Robert to hold a businessman or woman on their way to various jobs in the city. The people were unhappy. They were making money, living in nice places, driving nice cars, and they were miserable, sick in their hearts, in their bellies. They were living lives of strident desperation, public and still almost invisible. Yet, Robert saw. He saw the pain. He saw pain real well. Robert's 20/20 was a brown study, a blue apparition.

Now the agony in Robert's own head moved down his jaw. He could still detect crumbs of biscuit and sinewy pieces of meat in his teeth. On his right side, where he had masticated the spurious food, his teeth were coated in jellied victuals. The novocained side of his mouth. He had to clean it with a fingertip.

Robert rested on the good side of his head. The pain felt as if it spread across his damaged side like water over glass. Robert thought about going back to Walgreens to get some aspirin. But he didn't want to move. He was almost luxuriating in his silent misery, the traffic like some avant garde film about modernity. Or like a moving painting, the colors whistling by in impressionistic glow.

"You ok, Bob?"

Robert Walker moved only his eyes upward. Whiskey Dave stood over him. He was wearing a new coat, perhaps a woman's dressing gown, with a pink background and multi-hued flowers over it. Whiskey Dave put a hand on Robert's shoulder. Only Whiskey Dave called him Bob. That's not true. Lyn had called him Bob. Or Bobby. When she was being affectionate, on those demonstrative days.

Whiskey Dave was a short, compact man, powerful still, with strong arms and shoulders. He had been a promising semi-pro baseball player, a long time ago. A lifetime ago. He still wore baseball caps exclusively, and seemed to have an endless supply. He usually wore a Rhodes College cap but today's read Kansas City Monarchs.

Dave had been married once to a woman named Katelyn Sugg, a real beauty and a woman of great soul. Robert didn't know what happened to Dave's wife. Just one more of the burdensome secrets men and women carry like scars.

"Ok, Dave," Robert Walker said.

"Face hurt?"

Whiskey Dave had a sixth sense about such things.

"Little," Robert said.

"Have some whiskey," Whiskey Dave said. He held out a small bottle.

"Yep," Robert said, fumbling to an upright position. He took the bottle and tilted it into his mouth. Half the whiskey flowed into his beard.

"Dammit," Robert said, sputtering.

"S'ok," Whiskey Dave said. "More where that came from."

Robert tried again. By placing the entire opening of the bottle inside his mouth he was able to swallow a large gulp. It burned him but it was a good burn. He felt it moving downward, a beneficial blaze. Now Whiskey Dave was holding out a grimy palm. In it were two small orange pills.

"Ecotrin," Whiskey Dave said. "For the pain."

Dave watched closely as Robert tilted the bottle up once more, this time throwing back the pills at the same time. He managed to get them down without choking.

"Wife had the palsy once," Whiskey Dave said. "Helluva thing."

"Thanks, Dave," Robert Walker said. He already felt better. Though the pain still thrummed in his cheek.

"Want some breakfast," Whiskey Dave said.

"Had mine," Robert Walker said.

"Alright," Dave said. "Gonna hit the Walgreens lot and then maybe McDonald's."

Robert Walker grinned as well as he could. Dave

raised a hand in farewell.

"Thanks, Whiskey Dave."

"To be continued," Dave said.

6

ROBERT Walker stretched like a cat. The park was quiet. Only the sound of the traffic reached Robert's ears, one of which was acting like a wind tunnel, distorting sound. Robert needed a plan.

Then he remembered hearing about a new place in Memphis, a place where the homeless could shower, spruce up, have some coffee. It suddenly became the most necessary thing. What was the name of the place? Saint Dumpling House? That didn't sound quite right.

Though he didn't have the name in his head Robert Walker knew approximately where the place was. On Jefferson, between Midtown and Downtown, or in that vicinity. It would make for a nice morning's hike. He decided to cut across the park. To his left were park service buildings and Fire Station #13. He avoided that part of the park.

Robert entered The Old Forest on the path adjacent to his sleeping quarters. He eyed his secreted box as he passed it. He assumed that one night he would return to it to find it occupied. The homeless were like those crustaceans that make a home in any abandoned shell. Were they crustaceans? Or one night the cardboard cubby would simply be gone, another home gone.

The path was dark and quiet and damp. It felt good. The odor was rich like loam, like life going on under the surface of things. Robert breathed it in. One half of his nose tingled with the richness. The light that filtered through the trees, the early morning light, was like citrine refractions off water. Birdsong ricocheted around in the branches. The pain in Robert's jaw began to sing, also. A bright bloodshot song of impairment.

Deep into the woods Robert heard rustling, a human grunting sound, from just off the path. He knew what to expect. A couple, youngsters usually, using the haven of the darkened forest for their rutting. It would not be the first time he chanced upon lovers.

This morning it was two young men, lying among the rotting leaves and fallen limbs, both with trousers around their ankles. Robert stopped. He didn't know why he stopped. The movement of the white buttocks in the fuscy morning entranced him. Though Robert was heterosexual he was turned on by this surprising development. A half-smile crept onto his face.

The boy underneath had his face turned, half cushioned by a jacket. Robert could see his grimace of pleasure—and Robert felt it in his loins, too. The boy was Asian, possibly Vietnamese. Robert studied his face, wanted to understand his gratification. Robert was moved, standing in the cool dark morning forest. He kept looking from the face to the pistoning buttocks. It was like a magic trick, a transference of power and light.

Robert reluctantly moved on. Now his walk was sprightlier. Some kind of happiness had entered in. Robert almost forgot his pain.

7

FURTHER down the forest path Robert Walker came upon the rotting carcass of a wild pig. It was an odd thing to discover in an urban forest, so close to busy streets. But the park was also part of the zoo and Robert wondered if the pig came from the zoo.

He bent down to inspect it closer. It was bristly, dark brown and pink mottled. Its snout looked malevolent and Robert was glad he had not encountered it alive. It looked like it could do some damage.

How did it die? Robert wondered. There didn't seem to be any holes in the part of the body he could see, no blood in evidence. Robert was tempted to place his hand on the cold carcass. He squatted and inspected the pig as best he could. Should he tell someone once he got out of the woods?

"What did you do?" the voice came from behind him.

Robert Walker stood up quickly, a little too quickly, and he almost keeled over. The strange pressure in his ear was throwing off his personal gyroscope.

Robert was face to face with the Vietnamese boy he had just seen having sex. Robert was discombobulated, shy and a little frightened by the boy's sudden appearance.

"What did you do?" the boy repeated.

"Nothing," Robert Walker said. He tried a calming smile but it turned into a horrid contortion.

"You killed that pig," the boy said. It was not a question.

"No, no," Robert said. "It wash already here."

The boy squinted at Robert. He was trying to figure out his strange speech and odd mouth.

"You hungry?" he said.

Robert didn't understand the question.

"You hungry? You kill pig?" the boy elucidated.

"No," Robert said, simply.

"You kill pig," the boy repeated.

This time Robert didn't answer. He tried another smile with the same sad results.

"I tell police. You spied on me and then killed pig. I tell police."

Robert Walker decided just to leave the boy behind. Communication was impracticable. Communication was ineffectual. He turned and resumed his way down the path. He glanced back once and waved. No hard feelings. Sorry. Goodbye.

The boy stood next to the dead pig. He did not wave back.

8

Robert Walker emerged from the Old Forest onto the vividly lit smooth contours of a golf course. After the forest the golf course seemed overly showy, super-brilliant. It was like stepping onto a giant pool table. This early there were no golfers, few people in the park at all. To his right Robert could see the Art College. Some days he sat in the part of the park adjacent to the college and watched the brightly colored students going in and out. The boys were all urban punk but the girls were like confections: flamboyant, funky, beautiful.

Now, Robert Walker stepped through the dewy grass toward Poplar Avenue, a busy thoroughfare any time of the day, an avenue that ran from the river in the West all the way out of town and into Germantown, Collierville and beyond. Robert Walker had always hated Poplar Avenue. It was too narrow for its six lanes. There were too many uneven lanes. Automobiles, trucks, Hummers like inner-city tanks, bounced along as if in a bumper car concession. And right-hand tires kachunked into the gutters and scraped the curbs. It was madness, a sanctioned death race.

Now, Robert Walker did not have to worry about traffic much. He walked. Occasionally he heard of other homeless men and women being hurt or killed in traffic, wandering onto busy streets as if out of a past where cars did not exist, as if they were rushed upon by angry machines from the future. They walked right in front of cars and were knocked down and sometimes killed.

Memphis was not a pedestrian-friendly city. Monk Cassava came to mind. Wasn't Monk killed by traffic? He thought so.

He walked.

West along Poplar Avenue, out of the park, past the entrance to the Art College, past The Parkview, a retirement home, to the corner of McLean and Poplar where he veered left. On his right was St. Peter Villa Orphanage/Target House and a bit further, Catholic High School. Southward toward Union Avenue where he turned right and continued to head west. The switch to Union Avenue was strategic; there were more opportunities along the busy thoroughfare for handouts, for meets with others on the bum, for finds. Finds could be anything from a usable sweater to a half-eaten package of Ding Dongs, with one still untouched. Finds were a large part of Robert Walker's world.

There was also more opportunity for abuse. Often people threw things from cars. Teenagers with half a milkshake, or a can. Some of Robert's acquaintances called the cans a boon, some of the can collectors. Robert admired the can collectors but it wasn't his thing. Better to panhandle. Easier. Even if it put him in the same category as the gypsies and hitchhikers, the temporary homeless, who only stuck around for a week or two.

The local homeless set up a routine with area businesses and would do cleanup and odd jobs, which sometimes left the travelers high and dry. Also, the travelers were pretty much run out of downtown and forbidden from East Memphis, so they tended to all journey around midtown which made natural resources short in supply. Some midtown groceries had regular dumpster divers who stripped them of food. The local restaurants didn't hand out to anyone but their regulars. The travelers lived on the kindness of strangers and had a greater tendency to panhandle than the locals do. Yet, Robert didn't know the travelers, the gypsies, nor the local eateries, and they didn't know him. This was how Robert wanted it. He did not want to be known in too many places.

Now the ache in Robert's ear and jaw increased in intensity as if someone had turned a winch. Half his head felt inflamed. He held it with his hand, putting a finger over his eye to keep it closed, to keep the grit out.

Union Avenue traffic buzzed by Robert like the roar of neoteric, science fiction animals. The din hurt Robert's damaged ear. The sunshine stung his skin, seemed to enter his skin, penetrating epidermis to heat up his undercoat with electricity. Robert felt bad. He walked with a hand held to his cheek. Union Avenue was all fast food outlets and store fronts and churches. Robert knew the thoroughfare well. He felt at home on Union. A lot of bums did.

Outsiders, that's what Whiskey Dave calls us, Robert thought. Whiskey Dave used to be an actor and a radio deejay. And a ballplayer. Then he read a lot of books about bums and bindlestiffs and hoboes and railroads and decided he wanted to hobo for a while. And it just stuck. Whiskey Dave was the closest thing to a friend Robert had now among the Outsiders.

Next to the Starbucks, at the rear of an old house, was where Debra slept most nights. Debra who was beautiful once, who carried herself with grace and dignity, whose face still shone from beneath the grime and weathering like a peaceful star. Robert was a little in love with Debra but so was every other male on the street. Most felt protective of her so that she was relatively safe.

Debra also could not make understandable speech at times. She wasn't aphasic. She was extremely shy. So shy her brain didn't put words together in logical order, some thought. But Robert listened closely when she spoke and sensed that she was only so withdrawn because she didn't want to draw attention to herself or fill the world with empty blather. Talking to Debra made your heart ache. Talking to Debra put bees in your head and it was hard to forget her once you had engaged her in conversation. She wore her brunette hair like a veil. Or like Veronica Lake if Veronica Lake were duskier.

Also, Whiskey Dave told Robert Walker that Debra often went to Burke's Book Store, where they all knew her and showed a great tenderness toward her. But once, one of the well-intentioned clerks offered her a sandwich he had bought but wasn't going to eat. Debra flushed, grew confused, and fled. Later Dave found her a few blocks from the bookstore, sitting on the curb in front of Zinnie's Bar and Restaurant. She was crying, her weeping a quiet soughing like the sound the wind makes on cool, empty nights.

Today Debra was not there. She was probably at the soup kitchen at Grace St. Luke's. It was a popular spot for Union Avenue's bums. Debra was well-known there and Robert hoped that was where she was so that she was out of harm's way and taken care of. He toyed with the idea of heading down there himself but he had already eaten and he was in search of something else now, a shower, a clean-up, before he headed for the university. Robert had heard about this place—St. Dempster's?—from Debra.

He walked past Methodist Breast Center, The Fire Museum of Memphis, Schnuck's Grocery (Robert still thought of it as Seesel's, a family-owned store for decades), the gothic, fairy castle building of Idlewild Presbyterian Church. As Robert passed the now boarded up Midtown Video he caught a glimpse of someone he would just as soon not have dealings with. They called him Queeg on the street, because of his resemblance to Bogart's crazed and paranoid naval officer, but Robert knew his real name was John George. He had once been a bookseller, back in the days when bookselling was still profitable. Queeg had even owned a storefront, a small bookstore in the college area, which catered to students looking for cheap mass market copies of Melville, Dreiser, Faulkner, Kerouac and James Baldwin. Something had gone wrong. No one seemed to have the final version. Taxes weren't paid. The landlord was a greedy SOB. Queeg was caught stealing from the university library. Some said jail time was involved. All Robert Walker knew was that he didn't want to stop and talk to John George. The conversations were awkward at best, dangerous when Queeg's mind wasn't quite firing correctly.

9

"ROBERT," the voice hailed him from behind.

Robert Walker put a hand up to his painful ear, partly out of protectiveness, partly as a signal that he was busy, or that he wasn't hearing completely. Queeg never was one to pick up on subtle signals.

"Robert," he said again as he hied up next to him. He was out of breath after his ten yard dash.

"I didn't think you heard me," he said.

His face wore gin blossoms the way teens wear acne. And his hair was matted with something unspeakable. Even among the homeless he was especially unpleasant. Or perhaps these were Robert's perceptions, colored by the fact that he used to buy books from this man. He used to talk books with this man. For all his unpleasantness, for his entire disreputable aura, for all his seedy dishonesty, Queeg was a reader and a smart one.

"Where you heading?" he asked.

"Meet shomeone," Robert Walker said. Now Queeg took a closer look at Robert's liquescing visage.

"What the fuck happened to you?" he asked.

"Palshy." It sounded like pasha, or perhaps Porsche.

"Damn," Queeg said. He stood there staring at Robert in the early hours of the day, on the windy side of Union Avenue, across from a Wendy's, from which wafted the intoxicating aroma of French fries and grease.

The two lost men stood silently for a few moments longer. Robert wanted to say, Ok, you called this meeting.

Finally, he spoke, "Sauce do that?"

It took Robert a beat or two to understand.

"Uh, no," he said. "Don't think sho."

"Huh."

"Listen, Robert, listen. I need breakfast."

He said this as if this could be news among the itinerant.

"I've eaten," Robert Walker said.

"Got any spare?"

"No, no, naturally I don't." Robert couldn't keep the irritation out of his voice.

"Go with me. Down to Walgreens," he said.

"Can't," Robert replied.

"Uh huh." Now he brought his splotched face close. "Fucker," he fairly snarled.

Robert Walker turned to go.

"Fucker," he repeated. "I know you, Walker."

It had occurred to Robert, in the past, that people switch to your last name to show either affection or disdain. Robert didn't think this was affection.

"Don't forget. I know where you came from," he said. "Fucker!"

Robert Walker hurried away, pulling his thin coat about him as if it would protect him from the wind, the grit, the crazed, the human storm. Robert moved westward down Union. He passed Wiles Smith Drug Store, a Krystal, an Office Max, the Kimbrough Towers at McNeil. The Cupboard Restaurant. Robert felt himself excluded from his city, from Memphis, from life. He again debarred his dark contemplations.

10

ROBERT Walker sat down on a bus bench near Union and Cleveland. The traffic on Union was monstrous, clamorous and reckless and full of malevolence. But he was more concerned with the red, blistering pain on the right side of his head. He leaned against the bus stop's grimy plastic wall and shut his eyes. Whiskey Dave's Ecotrin was already wearing off. Robert was concentrating on where he needed to get and on not falling asleep. He dozed.

He awoke to find three people gathered around him in a semi-circle. They were well-dressed citizens of Memphis, Tennessee, and they were staring at Robert Walker as if he were an avant-garde art installation, or an exhibition in an autopsy hospital.

"He's opened his eyes," a woman said.

"Is he alright?" a man's voice.

"Looks crazy," the woman again.

"Something's wrong with him," the man answered.

"It'll be ok," the woman said. "We did the right thing."

"I think so," the man answered.

Robert was blinking at them, or at least he thought he was. Instead he was winking and drooling. His ragged, patchwork beard—a legacy of Native American blood he was told—held the drool like condensation in a spider's web.

"Don't you have anything to shay?" Robert asked the silent member of the trio, a woman about 25, with glossy auburn hair, and a bosom that could feed quadruplets.

"My," she said, not so much to Robert, but to the group. They continued to talk as if Robert wasn't there and soon Robert cottoned on to the fact that they had called an ambulance, or the police, or both. They have taken me for dead, or badly hurt, he thought. They had, because he was unconscious, and had slid down to a nearly prone position, his legs akimbo and stretched out before him on the sidewalk, and because his face was apparently liquefying.

Robert struggled to a more upright position.

"He can move," the idiot woman said.

"Maybe we shouldn't have called the police," the fretsome man said.

"My," the younger woman said.

Robert Walker grinned at her, the quiet one, but it must have looked horrifying because she was horrified. She put a hand to her brow, in imitation of a distressed movie heroine.

Robert stood up and looked about him. The sun was a burning lemon in the sky. Robert's eyes hurt. The trio took one lock step back but stayed with him.

"Thank you," Robert said, like a nincompoop.

"You're drooling," the young woman said.

"It's your tits," Robert told her and moved off. At Union and Cleveland Robert Walker headed South up Cleveland, away from Union Avenue and its well-meaning lunatics.

11

Now Robert faltered. He had gotten away from that embarrassing and awkward encounter but he lost his sense of purpose. The pain in his jaw and ear would have to be dealt with soon.

But now he stood still, looking down a somewhat bleak section of city sidewalk, carparks and parking lots and odd little storefronts. Medical buildings, some in use, some empty and desolate. A tavern perhaps. Robert felt that old thing going wrong again. That worm. He shook his head. He needed Whiskey Dave and his stimulants.

Then he popped back into real time. He wanted that place, the one he'd only heard tell of, the one where the homeless could not only get a bite to eat but a shower and a brush up. And he remembered why he wanted these things: Gayla Something. Gayla. Certainly an angel's name. And she looked angelic. Halo of lit-blond hair. Face of youth. Slim limbs and soft stomach. Where was Robert going with this thinking? He stopped the forward momentum of it. He would go to meet Gayla because she was nice, because she asked him, and because what else did he have to do?

What was the name of the place he sought? Daimler House? That didn't sound right. And he really only had a vague idea where it was. Whiskey Dave had told him but he couldn't remember. He had an idea what part of town though. Peabody? Was it on Peabody? Or perhaps Central. No, Central couldn't be right. Between Central and Harbert?

Up ahead Robert Walker saw Crump Stadium. He smiled despite himself. He was old enough to remember Crump Stadium, to have actually seen a game there, a high school jamboree when he was a teen. Robert sat down in the shadow of Crump Stadium. His ear was aflame.

The police car was beside him with its window down before he knew what was happening. Had he closed his eyes?

"What's up, Doc?" the black policeman said. He was smiling.

"Shorry," Robert said.

"Have you been drinking, sir?" The smile was fading.

"No shir," Robert Walker said. A small thrum began in his chest. He didn't like talking to the police. He always thought he was one wrong word from a jail cell.

Now the policeman slowly got out of his car as if every muscle in his body ached. It was really the infinite patience of the authority for the scofflaw. He had a mustache like the black cop on *Barney Miller*.

"Can you stand up, sir?"

"Yesh," Robert Walker said and rose.

"What's your name, friend?" the policeman said. A distant cousin of the smile returned.

"Robert," Robert Walker said. "Walker."

"Robert, your speech is slurred. Would you like to take a breathalyzer test for me?"

"No, shir," Robert said.

The policeman looked at him now with more compassion. He sensed something else was wrong.

"My speech," Robert said, sucking on his lower lip,

"it's the palsy." He got the word palsy out pretty well.

"Palsy," the patrolman said.

There was an uncomfortably long pause. The officer driving the car seemed to be thinking of something far away. The car hummed and popped and ticked.

"Bell's palsy," the officer now said. "My aunt had that. When did it start?"

"Thish morning," Robert said. He started to breathe a little easier.

"Would you like us to take you to the clinic?"

"No, shir, no thank you," Robert Walker said. Then, after a second, "You don't have any ashpirin, do you?"

The officer's smile was now quite nice. Robert wanted to stand and look at it for a while. The officer put a hand on Robert's shoulder and then got back in the car. Robert thought they were about to drive away but the officer got back out and handed Robert a bottle of aspirin.

"Thank you," Robert said.

"You're welcome, Robert. I've seen the palsy. Comes like an alien in the middle of a clear day, stays awhile and then leaves just as mysteriously. You'll be alright."

Robert now believed he would be. It was the voice of authority.

As they drove away the officer waved without a backward glance. Robert dry-swallowed 4 aspirins.

12

Robert Walker shuffled Southward against the wind. It continued to bedevil his bad eye. And his tongue began spasmodically licking the dead side of his mouth. He imagined he was quite a sight. He felt an animal shame. What a futz he must seem! What a simpleton! What an abnormity! No wonder most folks give the homeless a wide berth.

The aspirins began to chip away some of the pain. Robert's mind commenced to work against him. This is how it started, the bad thinking. This is how the devil gets in. That's what a therapist told him once, back when he was more whole than he is now. Why was he seeing a therapist? He had to ask himself and he had to think about it seriously. Why? Then like a storm his head hurt. The pressure began behind his nape and shot upwards like a spike. Black thoughts swelled like tempest clouds. He couldn't think about it. He. Could. Not.

Lyn's face then. Lyn was so pretty. Robert loved how pretty Lyn was. Is. She has strawberry red hair and a pale complexion and freckles across her nose and cheeks like a little girl. Lucid blue eyes, sharp nose. A small mouth, a mouth so small she had to use a child's toothbrush or she gagged. Why she couldn't do some things Robert liked done. Even French kissing sometimes made Lyn tense, or uncomfortable. Robert wanted to think about Lyn's face. His mind began to slow some. The bad things edged away.

Where was Lyn today? What was she doing? Robert thought of her often. Did she wonder where he was now? Did she care?

Fruitless probing.

As Robert gathered wool he also made progress, walking. He was trying to remember the name of the place he was going. Not Pilgrim House, or Nightingale House. Something House. Eddie House. No. Who is Eddie House? No, it was a saint. Not Jude. That one was taken. St. Jude, patron saint of lost causes and cases despaired of.

Lyn.

13

Robert wobbled a bit as he slowly made his way up Cleveland, a planet on a skewed axis. He was unsure of the cross street. Vinton. Harbert, as in Harbor?

His step slowed. He swayed like a bird on a twig. His earache was a dull throb. He closed his eyes hard but his damaged one stayed ajar. Suddenly, he was aware that a car had pulled alongside him, matching his slow progress.

Robert Walker turned toward the car. It was a beat-up Pinto, the orange of Pokey. Inside were three young men and two of them were hanging out windows, grinning like enchanted apes.

"Say, Gilligan," one spoke, a scraggy looking white kid with hair like boar's bristle and no chin. "Where ya goin'?"

Robert was sure that telling the truth was the wrong thing, a miscalculation.

"I don't know," Robert said, telling the truth anyway.

"Gilligan doesn't know," the kid said.

A young black man hung out the front seat window. He had a face like a black angel, round and shining and full of delight.

"That right, fuckweed?" the black angel spoke.

Robert's heart fluttered. This didn't seem right at all. He tried turning away, turning his back to the Pinto. They stopped the car and the two speakers got out.

"Say, Gilligan, since you don't have a destination maybe you could ride around with us. Whaddya say?

We've got some killer weed." The kid's expression was phony-friendly and as full of malice as a cobra about to strike. Robert felt as if he were about to be struck and his chest smarted with coiling anxiety.

"No thanksh," Robert Walker said and approximated a smile.

"What the fuck is wrong with you?" the black angel said to him, stepping closer, practically standing on Robert's feet.

"Palshy," Robert Walker said.

"What you call me, dickhead?"

Robert stepped away and as he did both boys grabbed his arms. One of them dug his knuckles into Robert's kidneys.

"Pleezhe," Robert said.

The white kid popped Robert on his sore ear. The pain buckled him. And as he buckled the two hoods roughly pushed him into the car. Robert was half-prone in the backseat. The white kid held him in place with a forearm. A panic was growing in Robert like vomitus, the panic of being inside a car.

"I—I can't ride—" he began.

"You stink, old fella," his captor said.

"Drive," the black angel said, getting back into the front seat.

"Whatcha doin,' ducky?" the driver said.

Now Robert was aware of her. The driver was a girl, sixteen or so years old, and as pretty as Rosanne Arquette. Robert only saw the side of her face, half hidden by a mop of reddish-brown curls. Her smile was loose, her eyes swimmy. She was driving but she was also flying.

"You lookin' at Rosy, Mr. Hobo?" the black angel said. "You fancy Rosy? Maybe we can take you some place and let you play with her?"

Rosy tittered. It was not the titter of a beautiful woman. It was the sound a rat might make before sex. The white kid pressed Robert's face into the seat. They drove on.

"No, I," Robert started to say.

The kid punched Robert again on his sore ear. The pain almost sent Robert into cuckooland. It was the birth of a star in his head. He saw constellations but he could still hear the ugly, vicious chatter around him. They were passing around a joint the size of a cigar.

"Don't think about Rosy," the kid said.

"Let him think about her," the black angel said. "He's probably horny as a dog."

"He can't have Rosy."

"Hell, you say."

Rosy tittered.

"Rosy, you don't want this old man, do ya?" the kid asks.

Rosy tittered.

"Rosy, she's a good girl," the black angel said. "Rosy likes men."

"I do," Rosy revealed. Her voice was like liquid glass.

"Lishen," Robert said, "I—"

"Can't hear you," the kid said, and he hauled Robert upright. The sun burst behind Robert's eyes.

"Listen," he started again.

"Take a look at Rosy," the angel said.

"Can't—" Robert Walker started.

"He can't see our Rosy," the black angel said. "Stop

the car, Rattlebrain."

Rosy tittered. And slowly pulled over to the curb.

"Let's stretch our legs," the black angel said.

The white kid grabbed Robert by the collar and pulled him out of the car. The unexpected momentum sent Robert to the curb where he skinned the palms of his hands. They were on an inner city street in broad daylight next to a rundown house with a "For Sale" sign out front. The house looked like the house in *The Ghost and Mr. Chicken.*

The two boys held Robert under his arms and dragged him toward the dilapidated porch of the house. They set him down on the top step and they sat on each side of him, up close, pinning him with their bodies.

A tear ran down Robert's cheek from his palsied eye.

"Don't cry, Mr. Bum," the black angel said.

The white kid laughed and his laugh sounded like someone sharpening a spear.

Rosy stood at the bottom of the steps, one hand on her hip, her body cocked like she'd seen models do in magazines. It was beautiful. It was horrific.

"Say, Mister," she spoke now. "You're a handsome man for a crazy. You ok?"

Robert looked at her. She had the body of a swimmer, large shoulders and rounded breasts and limbs like a silkie. Robert's broken heart broke.

"Yesh," he managed.

"You fancy our Rosy?" the black angel said and he elbowed Robert almost gently.

"No, no, I," Robert said.

"She too ugly for you?" the white kid asked. His features were bunched in the center of his face like a cavy.

"Sheesh beautiful," Robert Walker said.

"That's it," the black angel said. He stood up and simultaneously pulled Robert to his feet.

"Come here, Rosy," he said. She skipped past them, up the cold concrete steps and onto the porch whose floorboards were spattered, crisp and cracking.

"Show him," the angel said.

Rosy ducked her head for a moment. For a moment Robert thought there was some humanity in the scene about to unfold, some glimpse of vulnerability and heart. Rosy's eyes were pinwheels of narcosis. Then Rosy unbuttoned her shirt and unhooked her bra. She put her hands on her hips in a stance of challenge.

"Huh huh," the white kid said.

"How about that, Mr. Half-a-face," the black angel said.

Robert shouldn't have looked at her young breasts but they were the only thing of beauty in this miserable place. Now Robert quietly cried with both eyes.

"Open his pants," the black angel said to the weaselly white kid.

"Huh huh," the kid said and reached for Robert's belt.

"Pleesh," Robert Walker said. But the kid already had the belt unbuckled and his pants unsnapped.

Then a voice came, seemingly from the hedge beside the porch, a voice out of nature, a voice both human and godlike.

"What are you kids doing up there?" it said.

"Fuck off," the black angel said, but Rosy was already putting herself back together.

The four of them stood still for a few moments. The atmosphere crackled with uncertainty. It was like the abrupt end of a party slowly dawning on drunken guests.

"Fuck," the black angel said and he punched Robert one more time. Robert went down and as he did he could hear them running away. He could hear their crappy orange Pinto pull away. Robert didn't move for several minutes. Robert Walker wished he had died.

14

ROBERT decided to lie doggo for a while. Perhaps someone would come along and comfort him. Perhaps someone would bring him a pillow, a pill, a cup of sustenance. Perhaps a neighborhood cur would lick his wounds. Perhaps the world would leave him alone and Robert could quietly expire.

After a while Robert stood. There was a scratch and some small debris on his cheek. He could feel the small sting of an open abrasion. His hands stung. Also, Robert had to do up his fly. He sat on the cold concrete steps of the house for a while. The day had a mocking, light tangerine color to it. Robert hung his head. He knew that soon he would stand and when he stood he would hurt and still he would gather himself and walk on. He had forgotten his day's plan. His face hurt so he took some more aspirin.

Robert stood. The day moved around a bit. The sky swung. Robert reached out for a handhold and found the porch's column. He shook his head. The palsied side felt funny, like a drawing that someone tried to smudge out. In his mind it felt that way. His head was full of tumbled rubble.

Robert squinted at the somewhat bleak Memphis street on which he found himself. It was just off Cleveland, wasn't it? Robert walked in what he thought was an easterly direction. Something stopped Robert's progress, a peripheral vision. He turned his head to the right. There was a house there. The house had a sign

Robert Walker

out front.

The sign said St. Dymphna's Mission.

It rang a bell. This was not a house. This was a mission. This was where Robert had been heading, the place he'd heard good things about. What obscure sortilege led him here? He trundled across the street. The door was painted a welcoming cobalt, the color of the sky after the rain, a pluvial blue. Robert stood before that door and wondered how bad he looked. He decided here it did not matter. This thought comforted Robert Walker, whose day, so far, had not been very lucky. He went in.

15

INSIDE it was bright and clean and colorful. Robert expected a waiting room like a doctor's office but there was no desk or obstruction, no Cerberus to prevent one from simply walking in and walking around. There was a wide hallway, bright and lively. There were people going places, bright and lively. Robert stood diffidently near the door and surveyed. It was a little intimidating because it was new. Because everyone there was already comfortable.

Then a woman approached. She was smiling. She did not wear a uniform. Robert discovered he expected a uniform. She was pretty, early 30s, thin but not overly so. Her hair was a beautiful pile of muddy curls. Her hair reminded Robert of staring at the Mississippi River, hypnotized by the small eddies and wavelets.

"Hello," the woman said.

Robert nodded. He was asudden self-conscious about how he looked. His abrasions, his dirty clothing, his melting visage.

"I'm Erin Pound," the woman said.

Robert took her slight, soft, white hand in his dirty paw.

"Robert," he said.

"Welcome, Robert. Are you hungry?"

Robert was hungry but he was having lunch with the woman from McDonald's. What was her name? Gretchen? No, Gayla. Her name was Gayla.

"No," Robert Walker said.

"Would you like to take a shower? Have your clothes brushed up?"

"Yes," Robert said.

"Good then."

"I'm. Thish. I haven't been here before."

"Ok," Erin Pound said. "Come this way."

She moved gracefully through a door that swung both ways like in a restaurant. Robert Walker followed her.

"The showers are at the end of the hall," Erin Pound said. She smiled a crooked smile. The crooked smile broke Robert's heart. He loved this woman. Her smile made her cheeks bunch like fresh fruit.

"There are changing rooms, just here," Erin Pound said, gesturing to right and left. "Would you like to see the doctor, also?"

"N—no. No thank you."

"I'm not prying, Robert, but what happened? I really think perhaps a doctor might be necessary. Doctor Dan isn't here right now but he usually comes early afternoon. How does that sound?"

Robert was happy standing in the privacy of that little hall talking to Erin Pound. Her eyebrows were beautiful. Her voice was warm and brown like her hair.

"Can't," Robert said.

"Ok. Do you want to tell me what happened? I am one of the counselors here and we could have a little chat after your shower."

"Yesh," Robert said.

Robert went into a small room that was not as private as he had anticipated. There were two other men in there. They were both sitting in chairs and both were wrapped in large towels. One was as drunk as a boiled owl. The other was Pete the Hunchback. Pete was telling the near comatose man a story about a kangaroo.

Robert Walker

16

THE water in the shower was hot, a delicious needle-pointed sting. Robert imagined it was literally needles, small hot acupuncture pleasure on his shoulders. The shower stall was small with two nozzles to accommodate two people at once. Luckily, Robert was all alone and he luxuriated in that moment, letting the heat and pricking heal him, his lacerations, his sore ear, his groggy head now too full.

After soaping his head and getting under the water to rinse off Robert practically howled with pain. The soap ran into his open eye. It felt closed but it was not closed. The pain was like a small starburst in his face.

Reluctantly he left the shower and toweled off. When he found the changing room again Pete the Hunchback and the drunk were still in there. The drunk was singing what sounded like "Ob-la-di, Ob-la-da," but it could have been "Rhinestone Cowboy." Pete smiled at Robert and Robert sat down next to him.

"Aren't the showers amazing," Pete said.

Pete was one of the sweetest men on the street. He had had a hard go of it. Abandoned as a child because of his deformity Pete spent much of his youth in reform schools and then prison, where the taunting and the ostracizing were especially cruel. Now in his 40s Pete looked 60 but he never lost his smile.

Also, Pete always wore too many shirts and, affixed to the top one, a plethora of pins or buttons, some political, some inane. "Impeach Tricky Dick." "Frodo Lives." "The moral majority is neither." "Gene Rayburn for Pope." "Abbie Lives." "I dwindle." "War is good business. Invest your son." "We still have a dream." "Free Leonard Peltier." "Make coffee not war." "Grasshopper Lives." "Lysdexia." "I used to be disgusted but now I am amused." "Fleming's Fine Furniture." "A girl's best friend is her mutter." "Do I have enough flair?" "Free Willy." "I Go Pogo."

"Don't you feel like a million bucks?" Pete continued.

"Maybe a hundred, hundred-fifty," Robert Walker said.

"Ha, you're a man with a joke," Pete said. Pete sat laughing with small chuffs like a kettle just boiling. His small body vibrated with his chuckling.

"Whoozh your friend?" Robert asked, nodding toward the fuddled fellow on a nearby couch.

"Say, Robert," Pete said, looking more closely at Robert. "What's the matter with you? You had a stroke or something?"

"Some kind of palshy," Robert said.

"Polshy?"

"Pal—see," Robert managed.

"Palsy, Oh, yeah. I know that. Some kind of palsy. I'll be damned, Robert. I'll be damned. Does it hurt?"

"Ear hurtsh like hell," Robert said.

"Huh. Palsy. And it makes your face bleed, like, you know, the HIV thing?"

"No, no," Robert said. "I got beat up."

"Fuckers."

"Yeah."

"Street life. Sometimes I hate the street life."

"Yeah."

Now the drunk stirred. He opened one eye.

"Romans," he said.

Pete snuffled another laugh into his sleeve.

"What's the word, gents?" the guy said, slowly bringing his body to an upright position. It was an arduous process.

"Waiting for showers," Pete said. "Well, I am. Robert here had his. I had some of the soup and now I am waiting for a shower. They give you fresh clothes here too, if you want."

Pete's answer was apparently too involved for the guy to follow. He fixed Pete with a squinty stare.

"You're a hunchback," he said.

Pete snuffled some more.

"And you—hell's bells bells—I dunno what you are," he said to Robert.

"Robert. Robert Walker."

"Pete," Pete said.

It took a moment for the names to register. Names were being exchanged. Now the fellow seemed to shrug himself into his clothes. He made himself ready to speak.

"Sam Kerr Elm," Sam Kerr Elm said.

"That's a name," Pete said. He smiled like wine and roses.

"It's all mine," Sam said.

"Nicshe to meet you," Robert said.

"Had that," Sam said.

"Say what?" Pete said.

"Had what poor Bobbert has. The AIDs. Had it once," Sam said.

Robert and Pete looked at each other.

"Naw, friend," Pete said.

"Had them all. Had the gooseberries and the walleye

and the shimmy-shakes. I been so long in hospitals I changed my address. Know what I mean?"

Neither Pete nor Robert knew and neither wanted to hazard a guess.

"It's like that thing," Sam elucidated. "That thing where you feel ok for a minute and then the floor hits you hard. Been that done there. Know what I mean?"

Robert and Pete glommed now to the fact that it didn't matter if they knew what Sam meant.

"Raised out there, you know? Outside the walls? Know my way around. Been up, been down, been spun all around. Life's a monster, right boys? A monster. It's like that thing."

Robert and Pete waited. Perhaps now a response was expected.

Then Sam finished up. "You know, how the head of a chicken will run around after you've cut off its body."

The three men now sat together in silence as if at church. Light the color of gamboge came weakly in one shaded window.

Then Erin Pound returned.

17

ROBERT was made happy by Erin Pound's face. Her smile was like flute music.

"Robert, I think I found some clothes that will fit you. Wanna come see?"

Robert leapt to his feet. He would follow Erin Pound anywhere. Pain shot through his jaw, pain like the crack of a pistol.

He looked back once. Sam was picking something off Pete's shirtfront.

Erin and Robert went into an adjoining room. It was about the size of a changing room in a department store. It was a changing room. Robert was ready for change.

When Erin looked at him he gave her half a smile, a grin like a dog gives when its lip sticks to its teeth. She was holding up a dress shirt the color of a robin's egg and a pair of Levis, thick denim, stiff with starch. On the chair Robert's clothes looked like a collapsed tatterdemalion.

"We brushed up your clothes but thought, perhaps, you could use a clean pair. We've got socks, too. No shoes, I'm afraid."

"Fantathtic," Robert said and tried another lopsided smile. "I don't have any money," he added quickly, embarrassment suddenly springing with a flush to his ravaged face.

"No money accepted here," Erin Pound said. She smiled. Robert's heart moved closer to the hearth.

"I—" Robert said, but he had nothing else.

"You go ahead and change. If the pants don't fit I think we have some others. Would you like a sandwich or some coffee?"

"Water," Robert said, quickly. "Um, and coffee."

"Be right back," Erin Pound said.

Robert pulled the fresh clothes on. He had no underwear. He hadn't had underwear in days, maybe longer. The shirt caressed him, the pants softened against his chilled body. The clothes felt like tenderly rendered blankets. Robert sat down in the chair. He was close to tears.

Erin rapped lightly on the door.

"Ye—come in," Robert said.

Erin Pound held a small cardboard tray, the kind you see at fast food places. A water, a coffee, some creamer and sugar were there. She set the tray down on a small table.

"Let's see," she said. "Stand and let me see the fit."

Robert reluctantly rose. He was suddenly very tired.

"I think that's fine, don't you? Are they comfortable?"

Robert sobbed suddenly, a fish out of water.

"Oh," Erin said. "Sit. Sit."

Robert slumped back into the chair and cried into his hands. Erin Pound pulled up a chair close to Robert and sat quietly. She waited for him to raise his eyes.

After a few moments Robert did.

"Robert," Erin Pound said. There was a new weight to her speech. "Would you like to talk to someone here? We have a clinical social worker on staff. I might suggest you wait for the doctor, too."

"No, no," Robert snuffled. "I—I'm ok."

Erin looked intently at Robert's face.

"You're tho kind," Robert said. He leaned his face closer to hers. Erin jerked her head backwards.

"I'm thorry—" Robert quickly said. "Tho thorry." He put his face back into his hands.

Erin leaned forward again. She put a hand on Robert's shoulder.

"Robert, I'm sorry. This happens all the time. I understand. We're here to help you, ok? I'm going to let you sit by yourself for a while, ok? Get your thoughts together. Take your time. And then we'll have a chat in my office." She tapped Robert on the knee and she was gone.

Robert lifted his face from his scuffed and roughened palms and looked at them. He used to have beautiful hands. The only activity they had done was typing. Now they looked like the hands of a wild animal, abraded and scaly. Robert picked up his old clothes and took a deep breath.

He looked at the tray Erin had brought him. He put five packets of sugar into the coffee, stirred it and drank it down in one long swallow. It felt like fresh blood in his veins. Then he drained the water glass.

He exited the small room. To the right, down the narrow hallway, were the offices, the front door. Robert turned left and found a back door. It had a hasp and a combination lock on the inside but the lock hung open. Robert walked back out into the fresh air. Five steep, weathered wooden steps led down into an alleyway. There were garbage cans and a dumpster and further on a culvert surrounded by a chain link fence. Robert put his old clothes in the dumpster and moved off eastwards. He quickened his pace, putting a hand over his bad eye, as the breeze brought burning sand to his face.

Once around the corner and back onto the street he slowed his pace. He had to get to the college campus. The air went through his ear like a searing reproach.

Robert Walker

18

DOWN the street Robert Walker ran into Pete the Hunchback again. Pete was sitting on the curb fiddling with one of his shoes. He didn't look up at Robert's approach. Without preamble he said, "You'd think they'd have better shoes."

"What?"

"Pretty woman in there. Gave me these shoes. I think one has a burr in it, or maybe it's a jellyfish. You ever been stung by a jellyfish, Robert?"

"No, Pete," Robert said.

Pete squinted up at Robert.

"Where you heading, Robert?" Pete asked, with a whiskery tilt.

"College."

"That so?"

"Yes, I—"

"I went to college, Robert. Wouldn't you know? Went there, did some classes, did homework for those classes, saw some pretty pretty women. You ever see college women, Robert?"

"Yesh, Pete," Robert said.

"Best lookin' women in the world. Got their—what? – backpacks, knee socks, checkered skirts. Yum. Chased me some of them in my time."

"Yes."

"What you studying, Robert?" Pete squinted up at him again. The problematic shoe was secured with a Gordian knot.

Robert didn't know where to go with the conversation now.

"Meeting shomeone," he said.

"College girl?"

"Um, yesh."

"Best lookin' women in the world. Little short checkered skirts—"

"Right. Gotta keep moving," Robert said.

"Care if I tag along? Got nothing till my evening meal," Pete said. He made it sound like a dinner engagement at the mayor's house.

"No, fine, could use the company," Robert said, reluctantly. Robert liked Pete but, right now, conversation was coming kind of hard to him.

Pete put the shoe on. It was unclear whether he got the jellyfish out or not. He stood and stretched like a cat. His twisted little frame came up to Robert's shoulder, upon which Pete placed a hand to steady himself.

"Let's go, mate," Pete said.

They walked easterly down the timeworn city street with its old fashioned lamp posts and broken sidewalks. Pete was quiet for a while and Robert was thankful.

"Say, Robert," Pete now said. "Whatsa matter with your face? You had the stroke?"

"No, no," Robert said. "I don't think sho. Palshy. Something palsssy." Robert tried to elongate the sibilant syllables to sound less like a slur.

"I had the poshy once," Pete said. "Mean little disease. Made this hump you're looking at."

Robert decided that perhaps silence might be the best way to travel with Pete.

Robert Walker

19

AFTER the two men traveled some way in silence Pete glanced sideways at his friend. It was apparent Pete was pregnant with speech, with questioning.

"Say, Robert," Pete began. "You been slurring your speech today. Did you know that?"

Robert smiled kindly at Pete. What to say to satisfy him, to end the interrogation?

"Yesh," Robert said. Then added, with effort, "Yesss."

"Oughta see a doctor," Pete said.

Robert kept walking. The sun was high in the sky. Robert began to despair of making his lunchtime appointment. If he quickened his pace he would have to leave Pete behind.

Robert stopped. He pressed the butt of his hand against his offending eye. The pain there was coming back, seeping into him like shrill electricity. He fumbled in his pockets for the aspirin only to discover he had left them at St. Dymphna's, in the dumpster with his old clothes.

"Pete," Robert said now, looking at his diminutive friend. "I have someplace to be and soon. I am gonna have to increase the pace and, I'm afraid, part with you now."

Pete thought about this for a moment.

"We'll thumb a ride, Robert," he said.

"No—" Robert said quickly. "No, Pete, I mean, I can't take a car. I have to do it on foot."

"Helluva hitchhiker, Robert. I can stop a car. You

ever see that movie? I can stop them like that. It's the hump or something. I can get us a ride."

"Why don't you get a car for yourself?"

"Where you going, Robert?"

"I have a lunch-appointment."

"Gotcha, gotcha. You got a gal across town. You know that song? You got a...," Pete drifted away. "Gal. Sal. A gal for Robert. Woman."

"Right, Pete. So, sorry. We'll catch up later."

Robert hurried off. He glanced back and Pete was still standing in the same place. He seemed to be saying, "woman, woman, woman," to himself, like a man trying to sing his own lullaby.

Robert made a quick jog south at the next intersection. He wanted to find Central Avenue, a good walking street, and a direct line to the college campus. Robert hustled up the street, the wind around him like a swarm, a swaddling intensity.

20

ROBERT Walker made good time heading east on Central. It was mostly old sidewalks and older homes, some grand, some modest. The sylvan setting, green lush lawns, triggered old feelings in Robert, feelings he tried to keep tamped down. The Cathedral of the Immaculate Conception and its school where Priscilla Presley went. In front of it sat a young couple, dressed in black, the boy sporting a ten inch Mohawk, as elaborate as a carving.

Down a ways the houses sat well back from the street, pale palaces with shrubs cut into topiary elegance, a boxiness to their grandeur. Homes with wide sloping lawns, glistening green, as smooth as small green lakes, leading up to brick structures from the 1920s, with porticos and porte-cocheres and guest houses in rear. Leaded glass windows that would open, leading to rooms furnished in dark wood, rugs so plush you were soundless walking on them, crystal on surfaces, crystal in the light fixtures, shining little mirrors and light refractors. Robert put a hand to his temple. Lyn. Lyn in summer clothes, her leg slung over the arm of a wingback chair in just such a room, her white cotton blouse thin as gossamer, left open enough to show her rich cleavage, freckled, and her strawberry blond hair falling across her shoulders, her mouth in half-smirk amusement. Lyn. Robert stumbled forward a few steps. The sun. Somehow it had gotten hotter.

Once Robert had snuck up one of these sloping grass swards and stolen a drink of water from a garden hose. It reminded Robert of his childhood in Memphis, the warm, rubbery-tasting water rolling into his mouth.

At the corner of Central and Cooper, against the wall of Toad Hall Antiques, Robert sat. He had grown winded hurrying. Across the street Midtown Nursery looked like a small Eden. Between the green hanging plants and chain-link fence he thought he saw Debra's soft brown face but he couldn't imagine what she would be doing there. He said a silent prayer that she was ok and he hoisted himself back onto his feet and continued his trek.

"Say, Robert," a voice hailed him. He turned and saw Bowdre and his girlfriend, Bronwyn. She was Australian and as beautiful as a new pack of cards. Bowdre was almost an architect once upon a time, until he got deathly ill and his insurance company canceled his policy because they called whatever he had a pre-existing condition. In debt and without rent money he cracked up and began spending his days outside the State Farm offices, shrieking about what a grubby racket insurance is. He ended up suicidal and met Bronwyn on the 13th floor of St. Joseph's Hospital, the suicide ward. Even her five mile stare could not obscure the beauty of her eyes.

Bowdre was awkwardly toting a strange looking thing made of black wood and flexible metal rods. The wood was a sort of base and the rods spread out from it like a fountain. It was a little dingy and soiled.

"Bowdre, Bronwyn," Robert said.

"Know anyone buying art?" Bowdre said, a little breathless, a little panicky.

"Sure don't," Robert said and grinned at each of them to show he wasn't blowing them off.

"Found this. Can you believe it? Someone was throwing it away."

"It was in their yard, Bowd," Bronwyn said.

"It was at the curb," Bowdre answered sharply. Bronwyn just looked away. "I think it might be a Lon Anthony."

Robert just kept grinning.

"Ok," Bowdre said.

As Robert walked ahead he looked back to see the two of them struggling through the doorway of Toad Hall with their found art.

In Memphis, October can be quite pleasant. Most of the humidity is gone from the air and the city sits balanced between Spring allergens and Fall allergens. Robert's eyes were watering, meaning, perhaps, that mold spores were already at work. Plus, his one palsied eye smarted as if it had too much chlorine in it.

As Robert neared Central Barbecue he espied a female figure seated beneath its outdoor deck, poised on a cinder block chair. She had both legs tucked beneath her flowing dress, a feminine configuration no man could approximate or understand its lure. In her cocked right hand she held a cigarette as if it were a baton. Her whole attitude was elegant and poised and peaceful. She was as classy as Grace Kelly or Audrey Hepburn. It made Robert's heart ache. Then, as he got closer, he realized it was Debra. Her auburn hair shone in the weak morning light. How does it happen that Robert mistakenly saw her a block away and now here she was, as concrete as the Graceland gates? What is that called?

Some variation of déjà vu.

"Debra," he spoke, as he approached her. Robert was always conscious of how skittish Debra was, like a fawn. In her lap was a worn paperback copy of Iris Murdoch's *The Black Prince*. Debra always had a book. She must have recently been to Burke's Book Store. She scrounged change for $1 books the way some bums did for cigarettes and booze.

"Robert," Debra said, softly. It sounded like an exhalation, like an incantation.

"How are you?" Everyone's first question for Debra was, how are you? She was treasured.

"Fine," Debra said, ducking her head, hiding behind a russet curtain of hair.

"Howsh the book?" Robert said. He put a hand to his own cheek.

Debra squinted at Robert. She recognized that something was wrong but she was not one to initiate conversational tracks.

"Lovely," Debra said. She put both hands over the book in her lap. Her cigarette shrugged off some ash.

"I wish I could talk more," Robert Walker said. "I have lunch."

Debra smiled. She rarely smiled but when she did it was like sunshine on a polished apple. Robert started to pat Debra's shoulder in farewell but withdrew his hand. No one touched Debra.

Robert walked on. He glanced back once. Debra's cigarette was pointing skyward, standing upright from her dark, delicate fingers. Her other hand held the book open and Debra's concentration was like a child's at play.

21

Robert Walker had a vague idea what time it was. He was still walking into the sun so he knew it was before noon. He could make it to the U of M campus before noon if he were not interrupted again.

Crossing Parkway the noise and traffic beat on Robert's head like a simoom. He put a palm over the palsied eye. The sun felt good on his face. Robert quickened his pace. Past the fairgrounds—Robert still had a soft spot in him for the football stadium; he had had some nice dates there back when he was a young man—past the Children's Museum, and Tobey Park, Robert found himself again in a residential section. Stately homes set back from the street. One had a lawn as large as a pair of football fields. Robert wondered, not for the first time in his life, who could live in such a place, and how had they made that much money? How did all these people make that much money? A car honked. Robert stepped further away from the street even though he was safely on the sidewalk.

Robert began to feel a small upswelling of joyful anticipation in his heart. He began to feel good, walking in the autumn sunshine, even with his ear and eye and jaw raw and harrowing. And his new clothes were disguising him. He was, for a while, not an Outsider. He realized he had a bounce to his step. Though he must hurry he did not want to skip.

Robert Walker passed the rear of The Memphis Country Club, a golf course already enlivened by wealthy duffers. Once, he had been inside the club. It was something Lyn's family was doing. Now he couldn't remember quite what. He remembered finger food, though, little sandwiches made of air, cunning little vegetables and dip, a strong drink. Robert was overwhelmingly hungry. It had been a long time since McDonald's. He wondered if he would eat with this Gayla. He hoped she was buying him lunch but he wasn't sure and he fretted a bit about that.

Robert Walker was in a constant inner battle in opposition to memory.

He walked past spacious lawns, flatter here, so that the area between street and house looked like a well-tended infield. To his left was Chickasaw Gardens, an opulent neighborhood which had erected a brick wall so that it would not have to see too much of the surrounding city, its traffic, its people of color.

He passed The Pink Palace Museum. Robert remembered when it was entirely housed in Clarence Saunders's rosy stone home, when the chief attraction for him was the shrunken head, and the hand-carved mechanical circus. Sometimes Robert used to lose himself in that circus, imagine he was one of the small wooden kids in the stands.

At the corner of Central and Highland Robert stopped for the light. To his right was the Third Church of Christ, Scientist. Robert could picture his personal Jesus in a lab, making pigeons from earth and then smacking them back to dust. He realized he was breathing heavily. Was it anxiety or only fatigue? He rubbed the dead side of his face. Did it look as bad as it felt? Were the people in the passing cars imagining that they were seeing

Quasimodo strolling the city streets?

As the campus came into view Robert tried to remember exactly what the blond young woman had said. He was sure she invited him for lunch at the student center. Would that be easy to find? It had been a long time since Robert Walker had been on the University of Memphis campus. It didn't even have that name back then. Memphis State. That's what they called it.

Robert looked in wonder at the newer buildings, the Kemmons Wilson Holiday Inn Training and Management School, the school of music, the school of art.

Robert entered the campus with some trepidation. It had changed so much, especially on the Central Avenue side. There was more security, of course. Like everywhere else. Robert trudged up the smooth sidewalks, which wound through the green campus like snake paths. Robert experienced a sort of reminiscent joy, a body-memory. He was a student here. So long ago. And an English major, to boot. Now he was going to meet a woman who taught in that department. A beautiful woman, who looked like Gwyneth Paltrow.

Suddenly a most obvious question hit Robert. Why did Gayla want to have lunch with him? It stopped him in his tracks. Why had he not asked why before? Because he was carried away by her attentions toward him. Now he sat down in the grass. She had seen him at his worst. Just awake, palsied, smelling like a bum. She saw that he was an Outsider, surely. How could she miss it? Now Robert wondered if he should follow through on his promise to meet her.

On the winding sidewalks inside the campus, a meandering grey road through swathes of greensward and majestic trees, Robert spied Stan sweeping. Stan had been a fixture when Robert was a student there, decades ago. Now, he must be near 80, Robert thought.

Robert hailed him with a wave and walked over to him.

"Stan, how are you?" Robert asked.

"Good, good. Sweeping," Stan said. His lopsided smile was endearing, his unassuming ability to enjoy any activity. Robert remembered when Stan was an honorary batboy for the University baseball team. Perhaps he still was.

"You got your face all messed up," Stan said, smiling.

"I did, Shtan."

"It's Stan," Stan said.

"Yesh, I know," Robert said and he shook the kind soul's hand.

22

THE student center was a place of both chaos and peace. Beautiful young people, all weighted with books, crisscrossed in front of Robert, some headed to class, some to the cafeteria for lunch. The large, furnished study area seemed even more a place of splendor, angels recumbent on padded chairs and sofas, sneakered feet propped on coffee tables and coffee cups everywhere, in hands, on tables, resting on reclining stomachs. The scene frightened Robert yet he felt emboldened. The atmosphere was familiar to him. A nostalgic jolt of buoyancy went through him.

The cafeteria was loud and every table was taken. To further complicate matters there were two cafeterias. The odds of finding Gayla Calley seemed slim. Robert shuffled among the swarm. The wafting perfume of oily food almost knocked Robert down. He began to panic. The clock on the wall said seven minutes past noon. He had missed her. He was sure he had missed her.

Then, miracle of miracles, she was suddenly standing beside him. The radiance off her skin made Robert swoon. Her smile could break my heart, Robert thought.

"Robert," she said, taking his arm. "I didn't think you'd make it. I realized I should have offered to come pick you up. I have a car after all."

"No car," Robert said. It was not what he meant. It was not the first thing he wanted to say to Gayla Calley, though he had not prepared anything beforehand.

"Anyway," Gayla said, "Shall we get some food?"

"Uh, food, yesh…" Robert said. He was embarrassed.

"My treat," Gayla said in a low, confidential tone.

They went through the cafeteria. There were foods from all lands. Robert was intoxicated.

When they were seated, Gayla said, "You've got new clothes, don't you?"

"Yesh," Robert said, and suddenly he could feel his blotted shoes.

"You look very nice."

"Thank you." Robert Walker wanted to use her name but he thought better of it.

"Tell me, Robert. And you don't have to answer. Tell me how long you have been homeless."

Robert flushed red. He didn't want to talk about that. He didn't want to talk at all. He wanted to sit next to Gayla Calley and soak in her blond, cheering, rident presence.

"I'm sorry, Robert," Gayla said, quickly. "The last thing I want to do is embarrass you."

"What then?" Robert said. "What ish it that you do want from me?"

Now it was Gayla's turn to be embarrassed. She sat still but never took her eyes off Robert's face. She appeared to be weighing her options.

"It's not that I am collecting a forgotten man," she said. "It's just that, this morning, seeing you, disheveled and palsied, with your cheap breakfast, my heart went out to you. I can't describe it. I sensed that there was more story here than one might find with your average homeless person."

"*My Man Godfrey*," Robert said.

After a second Gayla laughed a rich, tinkling laugh.

"You know your movies," she said. "Forgotten man. I didn't even know from where I had appropriated that phrase."

She laughed again and this time Robert joined her. He was beginning to thaw. He realized suddenly he was holding a Reuben sandwich in his hand and, despite his roaring hunger, he had not yet taken a bite. He did now and the taste was sublime, triggering drool from the dead side of his mouth. He wiped his beard.

"You interest me, Robert Walker," Gayla said, after chewing a bite of her own sandwich. "Let's say, I sensed immediately a deeper stream underneath your red-rimmed eyes. I'd like to help you—if I can—If you want that."

"Thank you," Robert Walker said, around a half-chewed bit. He drank some tea, sweet ice tea with lots of ice. It was bliss. He also got coffee, an indulgence. "I really don't, uh—"

"What is it, Robert?" Gayla Calley put her sandwich down as if Robert had her full attention and was about to explain it all.

"I started to shay I didn't need help. But that's kinda abzhurd, ishn't it?"

"I don't know, Robert. Is it? Do you need help?"

"I do," Robert said. And then after a moment. "No, not really. I mean, well, you can see what my life izsh. It's just that, I can't, you know, be beholden…"

"Robert, why don't we just become friends and then we can see what's what? How does that sound?"

"Yesh," Robert said. And he felt safe and happy and peaceful. He took a sip from his coffee. Apparently even in school cafeterias the quality of coffee had improved.

This was a latte that actually tasted like a latte. Robert thought it was heaven. Whiskey Dave calls coffee "bum fuel." It's true. Like a cigarette to a smoking inmate, coffee to a street person is energy to get through difficult days. They both finished eating. And sat in congenial silence for a bit.

"Well, I have a class in 15 minutes. When shall we get together again?" Gayla Calley asked. There was that smile again, sun on a ripe pasture. "I can come pick you up."

"No," Robert said a bit too quickly. "I'll meet you."

"Tomorrow I finish classes at 11. How about lunch? What's close to you that you could make it?"

"The Cupboard," Robert said. "On Union."

"I know The Cupboard," Gayla said. "One of my favorite spots. A meat and three. When I was a student here, of course, it was Buntyn's, just down Southern. Student fodder. Good greasy Southern fried chicken."

Robert had a moment of discomfort, a memory trying to intrude on his tranquility.

"I'll be there," Gayla finished.

"Good," Robert said. He didn't want to be the first to stand up. He didn't want to leave her presence.

"And, Robert, do you want me to see if I can get someone for you to talk to about the Bell's palsy?"

"No, thank you," Robert Walker said. "It'll go away."

23

ROBERT had no idea where to go once he left the Student Center. His stomach was full, as full as it had been in weeks. He was vaguely aware of some lower level activity in his digestive system. This caused certain anxiety as always. He thought, perhaps, the easiest thing to do would be to go back into the Student Center and use one of their beautiful stalls.

Robert made a mime of forgetting something and went back up the steps, side-stepping students and textbooks, like a sapper. Inside, the air of the Student Center was oddly calming to him, like the oxygenated air they pump into casinos. Robert Walker felt healthy. He felt good. Even his jaw pain had diminished some.

Inside the immaculate bathroom there were a couple long-haired fellows smoking a joint over one of the sinks. Robert nodded at them but their faces showed nothing in return. Robert went straight to a stall and sat. It was liberation.

In his previous life Robert always carried a newspaper or magazine into the bathroom with him. It helped his natural responses and it made the loss of time less ineffectual. Now, he read the graffiti scratched into the hard surface of the stall's door and walls. Somehow he thought college students would be more inventive. There were a few clever scratches ("The road to good intentions is paved with hell" –Peter Devries), a few of the old, old language of scatology and futility and concupiscence. But, there in the middle of the door, at face-level, Robert read, "I stand up next to a mountain and I chop it down with the edge of my hand." Robert smiled.

After he finished his business Robert stopped to look at himself in the mirror. His face still looked pretty rough, seedy and unwell. The new clothes couldn't help that. His hands were weather-worn and his nails ragged. His facial hair looked sullied. There were morsels from his lunch captured in his beard like flies in a spider web. He cupped his hands under the hot water and was rinsing his beard when the campus cop entered. The song in Robert's heart missed a note.

Could those stoners have called security? This seemed unlikely to Robert though he knew no young people and their ways could seem unfathomable. Perhaps the new clothing was not as convincing a disguise as he imagined. Perhaps the stench of homelessness was on him, still, was in him, like a disease that manifested itself with outward deformation. Robert smiled at the officer. Water dripped from Robert Walker's beard.

"Hello, friend," the cop said. He was medium height with a big belly but his arms looked like they could strangle an orangutan.

"Hi," Robert said. Perhaps this conversation was not to be about him.

"You a student here, friend?"

"No," Robert said. He put a hand reflexively to his drooping cheek. "I was sheeing someone."

"Uh huh," the cop said. He was only a campus cop but he had obviously learned his patter from TV. "See some ID?"

Robert smiled weakly.

"You don't have ID, do you?"

Robert's smile straightened itself out.

"Come on," the cop said and he placed a hand on Robert's bicep. The grip was almost friendly, the pressure almost a caress.

"I really jusht had lunch here," Robert said. "With Gayla."

The cop looked at Robert as if Robert had said something inscrutable. "We've had some daytime rapes on campus," he said. "I guess you don't know anything about that."

Robert was horrified.

"I—I—shir, I, no, thish is my firsht time here in a long time." Robert was near tears.

"Let's go talk about it," the cop said.

24

THANKFULLY, the officer did not hold Robert Walker's arm in their march across campus. No one turned to look at them. No one spoke to Robert or the lawman.

The office where Robert was led was small and packed full of things as if there was once a larger office and it had contracted. Robert sat across a desk from the cop. He was reminded of the few student-teacher conferences he had sat through. The desk had so many untidy piles of paper Robert felt as if he were looking across a frozen stream of white. A spindle sat amid the heap like a spired buoy. The cop moved some of the papers around, opened a couple drawers, looked over his shoulder once or twice at wall space that surely gave no clues to anything.

"I had," he said, but the phrase died there.

Robert stirred in his seat. Pain was returning to his jaw and now most acutely to his ear. He tentatively touched his ear with a finger. The outside lobes were numb. Inside pain was spreading like a stream of arcing electricity.

"What's wrong with your face?" the officer asked, without looking up from his foraging.

"Bellz palshy," Robert said.

The officer stopped for a second. He looked at Robert's face.

"You always talk like that?" he said.

"No sir," Robert said. "Itsh the palshy."

"I don't know what pall—shee is."

Robert concentrated and said very slowly. "Bellz palzy."

"Oh," the officer said, and went back to his search.

"You got any ashpirin?" Robert asked.

The officer opened another drawer and found, surprisingly quickly, a tin of Bufferin.

"Thank you," Robert said.

"Somewhere I have the description of the guy," the cop said now. He sat back in his chair and surveyed the mess around him. "I really don't think it fits you."

Robert tried a smile, while simultaneously crushing two Bufferins in his teeth.

"Lemme make a call. You sit tight."

He got up and left the room even though there was a phone on his desk.

Robert put his head in his hands. He was suddenly so tired he thought he might sleep in the hardwood chair. Robert reluctantly lifted his head and scanned the room. Shelves on the wall held boxes of papers, a few paperbacks (Joseph Wambaugh, Leon Uris, a *Ripley's Believe It Or Not*, a *Farmer's Almanac* from 2004, a *Guinness Book of World Records*, a thesaurus), and some framed pictures of a homely, smiling family. The wait was interminable. He wondered what kind of ruse the officer was attempting. Possibly he just went outside so Robert could stew in his own juices for a while. Robert stewed in his own juices.

Memories tried to swim to the surface. Something to do with the family photo. Robert suppressed them. Robert was trying to live a life without memories. This was his definition of self for now. He was born 225 days ago, in a cardboard box, like a litter of kittens, hidden by ragged shrubbery and saplings and kudzu. He was born to heat and divestiture. He was born to loss, a child of loss. He was an Outsider.

Officer Andy Moon (Robert read his nametag for the first time) returned with a smile on his face and two cups of coffee. He handed one to Robert.

"Lots of sugar," Andy Moon said. "That's the way you folks like it, right?"

Robert Walker sat mum. The coffee was pure, hot righteousness.

"That's the way you folks like it, right?"

Apparently he wanted his egalitarianism acknowledged. Robert was trying to figure out what people he belonged to. Street People, that is what Andy Moon meant.

"Yesh," Robert said.

"What happened to your speech, Robert? I thought initially that you had been drinking. You can understand my mistake, right?"

"Yesh," Robert Walker said.

The men stared at each other over their coffees.

"Bellsh palzzy," Robert thought to say. They had already had this part of the conversation, Robert was pretty sure.

"Uh huh," Andy Moon said and took another swallow of his coffee.

"So, anyway, you don't match the perp's description. Lucky you, right, friend?"

Robert nodded.

"So, where do you go? Say, I just tell you to scoot. Where do you go?"

"Walk," Robert Walker said.

"Ok," Andy Moon said. He seemed to be at the end of his tether. He was out of ideas. So he waved a hand at the door.

Robert rose slowly. He put the Styrofoam cup down on the edge of the desk.

"Thank you," he said.

Andy Moon was already reshuffling the same papers.

25

ROBERT had nowhere to go but he was used to that. He was outside his usual comfort zone—Midtown Memphis—but decided to explore this part of the city, as soon as he could get off campus, where he stood out. The campus spread for miles. All around him were young people with intellectual curiosity. It made Robert ache. It also made him feel like the Time Traveler among the Eloi.

What he really wanted was to see Gayla again. He wanted her blond flame to dance before his eyes again. But he tried to suppress such excessive emotional—animal—expenditure. He tamped it down. He was used to tamping it down. Robert Walker walked.

When Robert got back to Central Avenue he looked left and right. Campus as far as he could see. He used to know what was East of there, stores and traffic and baseball diamonds and churches and homes for bankers and CEOs. He used to drive in East Memphis, on his way to the health food store, or to a movie. Beyond lay Germantown. It had been a long time since Robert was in Germantown. In retrospect Robert saw it as cacophonous and moneyed and frantic and congested. He did not want to venture that far, even if his feet could carry him that far. He didn't want that commotion.

What Robert Walker really wanted was to lie down and take a nap. Daytime naps were risky, especially in parts of town where he was not at ease. He could certainly end up in jail, or at least hassled again by agents of the law. Robert wanted to lie down and not think about the hot-knife pain in his ear.

Robert walked east down Central, dodging running students, huddling his shoulders up around his ears as if for comfort or protection. After the campus was behind him Robert once more found himself in a more residential part of the city, neat houses, neat yards, courtyards, patios, terraces, gardens. Up ahead was where Goodlett intersected with Central and did a hognose turn into Poplar Avenue, there at the Second Presbyterian Church.

But, on his right, Robert discovered the baseball field and soccer field he half-remembered. He was drawn there. The fields were peaceful in the sunlight, the wind kicking up little dust eddies around the pitcher's mound. Robert sat on the wee, crude bleachers and felt somewhat solaced. There was a peacefulness attached to sport, something that ran in Robert's veins. He remembered that Whiskey Dave had once played shortstop for the Memphis Blues, when they were a minor league team associated with the New York Mets organization. Dave played with Gary Carter. There were some homeless who thought Dave knew things not vouchsafed ordinary men. They thought Dave the Wise Old Man of the Forest. They heard of a wife, a life, a job, all abandoned because Dave worshipped freedom more than comfort. Dave was a mystery and not a mystery. He carried his wisdom and his magnanimity lightly. Dave was kind. Still the question persisted: how did Dave end up an Outsider?

How did Robert Walker?

Robert put his head down on top of his hands and in

that L position fell asleep.

He dreamt.

In his dream, which was lit by pearly gleam, neither night nor day but something in between, he was driving a car. A queer, viscous substance spread across the windshield as if it were raining grease. Robert couldn't see, and the road was a narrow, country lane. He could not make out the ravines on either side of the road, nor the ess curves, and the car seemed destined to culminate upturned in one of the ditches. Plus the car was going faster and faster and Robert could not slow it down. He let go of the wheel and began to cry.

"Mister, you ok?"

Robert blinked awake. Before his blurry eyes stood Little Bo Peep.

"Wha?" Robert said, half-sitting up.

"You ok?" the sprite repeated.

"I. Am," Robert said, blinking harder, though one eye refused to cooperate. He now saw the small figure was not Little Bo Peep but a freckled young girl, straight out of central casting, dressed in her Sunday School best.

"Yesh, yesz," Robert said, sitting all the way up. He wondered how long he'd been asleep.

"I thought you were sick or something. Your eye was open and you were crying and making little moaning sounds like my dog, Bowie, does sometimes."

"No, I wash, waz, dreaming," Robert said. He ran a hand across his face as if his features needed rearranging.

"I'm Manda," the blond sprite said, and stuck out a tiny, wan hand.

"Robert," Robert Walker said, taking the hand in a

courtly encirclement. "Glad to know you."

"You aren't sick, are you?" Manda asked.

"No, not really. My fashe—fface—is a little wonky. I have a condition."

"Uh huh," Manda said.

"What are you doing out here alone in your fanshy dresh?" Robert asked.

"I was at the church over there," and Manda pointed over her shoulder. "It's where I go to school, too, and today is picture day. I hate picture day and I wandered away."

"Why do you hate picture day?"

Manda scrunched up her little imp face. She seemed reluctant to answer.

"My face," she said now, looking Robert in the eye.

"Whatsh wrong with your face?" Robert said and gave a half-hearted chuckle. "It's better than mine."

Manda thought this over. "Mine's too freckly."

"Manda, you have a lasht name?"

"Kallen," she said.

"Manda Kallen, you're about the prettiesht girl I've sheen in a long long time. You are as lovely as a rill."

"What's a rill, a kind of monkey? Are you making fun of me?"

"I assure you not. It's a shtream, you know, a small tinkling river."

Manda giggled. The two sat looking at each other under the early afternoon sun.

"I guess I better go, Robert," Manda said. She had a gloss of maturity to her. It had slipped when she giggled but was now charmingly back in place.

"A pleasure," Robert said. He watched as she walked

away. His heart hurt just as if someone were inside him squeezing it with ragged claws.

26

R{ROBERT} decided not to continue East. That way led to the tony mall, the tony shopping center, the harum-scarum intersection of Poplar and Perkins, the overwhelming stimuli of Macy's. Robert made his way back west down Central. The wind had died down and the day was quite pleasant. Robert did not know what to do next so he moved back toward that which was familiar. It might not be too early to start begging coins for the evening meal.

He thought again of Gayla. Did she really want to see him again tomorrow? It seemed illusory, improbable. The last time he looked at himself he was not a pleasant package. Robert Walker gave way to distrust and its insidious partner, self-hatred.

And in thinking of Gayla, for some reason, Robert's thoughts returned to the woman at St. Dymphna's Mission. Erin, her name was. She was dark to Gayla's light. She was brunette and had beautiful eyebrows and a marvelous cockeyed smile, set off by cheeks as round as turnips. Where Gayla was Spring, Erin was Autumn. Robert felt an old vestigial tug. He fought it. It was better to be alone. The tug will always be with me, Robert thought, no matter how debauched my life.

At the corner of Central and Highland, as Robert Walker stood waiting for the light to change, he spotted that scoundrel Queeg jaywalking Highland to the south. Queeg crossed by half-running, half-skipping, holding up a forbidding hand to cars and cursing at them. He made it safely to the other side. Too bad, Robert thought.

Robert hustled across just in case Queeg looked his way. Down the shaded sidewalks of this upscale part of Central it felt almost cool. Robert thought about a better jacket than his bum starver. He could probably go to St. Dymphna's again for a coat. That was a good idea. And maybe some more aspirin. Maybe Erin would give him some more aspirin. The cop's still rattled in his pocket but he felt the need of an unending supply. Having them were a comfort.

Robert, back in Midtown, felt on solid ground again. He almost felt chipper, though he knew it was a fragile disposition. His soul sat on a teeter-totter.

Within an hour he was back in sight of St. Dymphna's. His heart rate was slightly elevated, perhaps only from walking so long. He approached the place somewhat boldly and went right in.

Inside it was calm and light and there was a quietude that was oddly reassuring. A young woman bustled up to meet him, a different young woman. She was plump, with an ample bosom and a smile that showed two dimples cut from her cheeks by a sharp, caring blade. Her hair was blond and sat on top of her like Harpo Marx's mop.

"Hi," she said. "I'm April."

"Robert Walker," Robert said.

"Have you been here before Robert?"

"Yesh," Robert said. "Jusht thish morning." His speech was getting worse. His jaw, his lips, were tired.

"Ok," April said, her face still bright like a blister.

"I—I wash wondering—is Erin still here?"

"She is," April said and stood there with a young

woman's smile.

Robert Walker did not want to talk to April anymore. "I'll get her for you."

Robert stood still, shifting his weight from foot to foot.

It took some time then Erin was deliciously there, striding toward him down the hall. She had those cheeks. She spoke his name. It sounded like flute music.

"Robert, what a pleasure," Erin Pound said. She gestured him into a small office off the hall. "Sit, please."

"Thank you," Robert Walker said. He couldn't take his eyes from her face.

"Everything alright?"

"Yesh," Robert said. "That ish … can I have some ashpirin?"

"Of course." Erin Pound reached into a pocketbook at her feet and after a moment pulled up a ring of birth control pills. "Oops," she said. Then, into Felix's magic bag again and this time she pulled out a tin of aspirin. "Here we go," she said.

Robert threw back four without water.

Erin Pound laughed. "Robert, I can get you some water," she said.

"Thank you," Robert said, and then added quickly as Erin rose, "and a coat."

"I'm sorry," Erin said.

"I wash wondering…if you had an old coat, a jacket, anything. It's getting colder."

"Oh, yes, of course. I'll find something." And then she added before opening the door, "There's actually someone here I'd like you to talk to. What do you think?"

"A doctor?" Robert said.

"Yes, that's right. Did I mention it before? Her name is Dr. Deidre Braun, but everyone calls her Dr. D."

"D ash in death," Robert said.

Erin Pound laughed. "What a funny thing to say, Robert." And she left him alone.

27

Erin Pound returned with a hooded Grizzlies sweatshirt a couple sizes too large. Robert held it against himself and smiled. It felt like some small consolation, for what he could not name. Erin took his hand—she actually took his hand—and walked him down the hall.

"Are you hungry, Robert? We start with dinner pretty soon."

"I am," Robert Walker said. And, in saying it, he unexpectedly was. He was ravenous. He was also happy to have Erin Pound's light, slight, slightly rough hand in his.

"I'll tell them you're eating with us," Erin said. "Right now, I'd like you to meet Dr. D. Is that ok?"

Robert smiled. He was suddenly tired of talking. And he really didn't want to talk to a doctor. Erin walked with Robert into a larger office, one with bookshelves on the wall, upon which sat numerous medical and psychology texts, mixed with popular novels. Robert knew some of the novels. He had read some of the novels. There were some Easton Press editions of classics. Robert thought, snob.

"I don't know where she is," Erin said, letting Robert's hand slide out of hers as if she were absent-mindedly dropping it. As if it were a book and she were falling asleep.

"I'll go find her. You sit here," Erin Pound said, gesturing toward a sofa.

Robert sat down. He feared what was coming.

Then, without warning, standing before him was a diminutive, dark woman with hair the color of coal ("black as incest," Robert had once read somewhere), and shoulders like a linebacker. She wasn't 5 feet 5 inches tall but she conveyed a haughtiness that immediately made Robert think of a prison guard. And she was dressed immaculately, right down to her dark silk hose. Her whole body tapered down to a pair of thick, squat legs on top of child's feet. She looked like an inverted pyramid, if a pyramid can look imperious.

"Robert," she said, extending a hand. Robert struggled to his feet. He was tired. He took her small claw in his hand. "Call me Dr. D," she said. She had a bluff cheeriness that was as false as a harlot's kiss.

"Sit, sit," she said.

Robert sat back down. He still had not spoken. His mind was working turgidly and his immediate dislike of this woman made him queasy.

"So, you have a little bell's palsy," she said, after positioning herself behind her desk. On the desk was an ingenious little fountain that constantly replenished itself, clear water trickling over fake rocks, which played a soft, new age music. Robert watched it for a few moments. He imagined there were people, maybe even people he encountered, who would find this little faux falls soothing.

Robert was silent.

"Robert, you, um, you perhaps need someone to talk to. This is why I am here."

Robert looked at his lap.

"Do you feel ok? How are you sleeping?"

Robert moved his shoulders almost imperceptibly.

"Your appetite ok?"

Robert was silent.

"Are you experiencing any suicidal thoughts?"

Robert was silent. Dr. D sighed in exasperation.

"You want to talk about your condition?" Dr. D asked now, a slight edge to her nursely cheer. "Can you tell me when you contracted it?"

Robert looked up. "I woke with it thish morning. It feelsh like a hundred dayz ago."

"You woke—where?"

"At my place," Robert said.

"I understood you are homeless."

It wasn't a question. She knew Robert was homeless.

"Yesh," Robert Walker said.

"So you don't have access to good medical care?"

"No."

"You might want to start with steroids for the palsy, yes? For starters. Cortisone perhaps."

"Mm."

"We'd like to help you, Robert. We'd like you to put yourself in our hands."

Robert sat stock still. His heart beat fast.

"It would only be a day or two. Perhaps three. You could rest. We could talk. You might have an underlying condition that the palsy sprang from. It might be stress. Would you say you've been stressed lately, Robert?"

"I live in a box," Robert said. His voice was icy. "Right now I don't have the confidence to complete a shtream of pee."

Dr. Deidre Braun stiffened. She studied Robert for a second.

"It is within my power to institutionalize you, Robert.

Did you know that? Would you like to be locked up for a while, maybe get some electric shock? Would you like that instead of talking to me, Robert?" She spoke like a Warner Brothers commandant.

Robert hesitated. Then he rose. He didn't know what to do next.

"I don't understand it. As long as I have been doing this, I don't understand it. We try to help. We are here to help. And all we get is rigidity, defiance. Where is the gratitude, Robert? Can you tell me that? Food taste alright to you? New sweatshirt—how does that feel, Robert?"

Robert put his hand on the doorknob. He felt a little faint.

"Oh, and Robert. 20% of bell's palsy victims suffer permanent damage," Dr. D said with a tight little moue.

"Goodbye, Robert. Sleep well tonight," Dr. D said.

Robert pushed out into the hall.

28

Robert did not want evaluation, drugs. He knew some outsiders who were sick. Schizophrenic meds have a tendency to sedate people to a large degree. Because of that a lot of people will stop taking their meds and end up on the streets. They just walk away from whatever paranoid ideation they are having or are kicked out by people who can't control them or who can't stand to be around them when they are spiraling down. These are the people who cycle through Memphis Mental Health Institute and 201 Poplar on a regular basis. Many of them have a little bit of a history with authorities and are on a first name basis. To the cops, a guy might have an intersection as an address, or a park or whatever is in his file along with his name. A lot of these people also qualify for disability but don't maintain an address long enough to receive help. They are brought in when they are off their pills and sent to MMHI or to jail or frequently to jail and then MMHI. They are fed and cleaned up and medicated until they are stable enough to go back to a group home or their family home or whatever. A lot of the long timers don't get picked up unless there is a bad scene that endangers someone or something and requires action.

Many of the homeless only wanted to be on walkabout, like Robert.

Robert thought he remembered that Dave said Debra had been through MMHI a number of times. Her exact problem was nebulous in his mind.

Robert headed for the exit. The tears in his eyes were causing diamonds to dance in his peripheral vision.

A voice called his name.

He turned to see Erin Pound hustling toward him.

"Where are you going? I was going to sit down and have some food with you. It's chicken and dumplings tonight. Mrs. Reid makes chicken and dumplings that'll make you giddy."

"Gotta go," Robert said.

"Wait, wait," Erin Pound said. "Sit here a minute and talk to me." She steered them toward a couch in the hallway.

"What happened with Dr. D? I thought she might have some good advice about your—your—damn, I can't remember what it's called."

"Bellz Palshy."

"Yes."

"She couldn't," Robert said. His jaw was set. His ear rang like a siren.

Erin looked in Robert's eyes. "What happened?"

"She wants to lock me up."

"What? Lock you up? I am sure you misunderstood."

"No," Robert said. He had to put his hand to his cheek. It throbbed harder than his heart beat.

"Robert, are you in pain? Take a couple more aspirin. And then we'll eat something."

"Can I shit here?"

Erin's face scrunched involuntarily.

"Szit," Robert struggled to say.

"Oh," Erin laughed a short laugh. "Yes, of course. May I sit with you?"

"Please."

"What did Dr. D really say, Robert?"

"She thought I was being shtubborn, shut-mouth. She told me I was unappreciative and that if she wanted to she could lock me up, electrify me."

"Jesus," Erin Pound said. She looked at her own lap.

"I'm sorry, Robert. You must have caught her on a bad day. She can be a bit—domineering. She doesn't like to be crossed. Or questioned. I can't say more. She really is a good doctor, Robert. She could help you."

"I never want to shee her again," Robert said. Then, unexpectedly, Robert Walker and Erin Pound began to laugh. The laughter was like gas expanding. It was cathartic. Erin put her hand on Robert's upper arm. They laughed like children.

"Shall we go see about Mrs. Reid's chicken and dumplings?" Erin said, as the laughter subsided.

"Thank you," Robert Walker said. And he smiled into Erin Pound's eyes, which were deep, brown tarns.

29

THEY didn't see Dr. D again. The cafeteria was really a largish room with a dozen or so card tables set up with folding chairs. The food was prepared in a small room off one side with a window cut in the wall between the rooms, just like in elementary school.

Robert Walker sat across from Erin Pound and couldn't take his eyes off her eyes and cheeks and mouth. He wanted to put a thumb against one cheek and pretend he was clearing off a smudge. The food was as good as Erin Pound said it would be.

Robert looked around. There were familiar faces, some friendly, some less. There were a couple of older guys, big guys who used to play football together for Ole Miss, who had roughed Robert up one night. Another table seemed to be all gypsies, travelers who were homeless by choice. Whiskey Dave said, they were not welcomed by the true Outsiders and often, they were shunned, but it didn't matter. They left markers around the city, bits of graffiti symbols that only they knew. And there was Kelly, sitting by himself, face hunched over the table. Kelly had psoriasis that covered his whole body and he was, at various times, molting like a bird. Everyone called him Kelly Green (or sometimes, cruelly, Grace Kelly) but Robert thought his last name was Norfleet. He was best known for having leapt from the Memphis Arkansas Bridge 3 times and lived. Three suicide attempts that failed. This made him something of a wonder, and a person of interest.

While they were eating, Whiskey Dave himself came in and, like a slow-moving shadow beside him, Debra walked along, head drooping, pretty chocolate hair hanging over one side of her face. Dave saw Robert and gently motioned Debra toward their table.

"Hello, Bob," Whiskey Dave said. "You know Debra. And who are you?" Dave put his hand out for Erin Pound to shake. Whiskey Dave never lost his courtly manners. "I believe we've seen each other before."

"Hello," Erin Pound said. "Erin. Hi, Debra."

Debra ducked her head even lower and she may have whispered her hello. Her hair was like a shady chestnut waterfall, underneath which, her weathered, but velvety skin shone. Her skin was the color of ripe figs but as soft as swan's down.

"Sit," Whiskey Dave said to Debra, and pulled out a chair for her. She sat, peeking out from under her veil, and smiling the way small children smile for Sunday school pictures. It was shyness but, also, perhaps she was afraid of talking daft. Dave went to get both of them a tray.

"Mrs. Reid deserves a Nobel Prize in culinariness," Dave said, after setting both meals down. "So glad to have food here with some of my favorite people. Better than the usual sinkers and joe at the mission."

There was hesitancy, mixed with admiration, at the table.

"Life is good," Whiskey Dave continued.

They all ate quietly for a while. Debra picked at her food.

At a table nearby sat an old black man with salt and pepper hair and beard, tending more toward salt than pepper, and wearing a pair of overalls that looked like they should have given out three owners ago. His plate was half-eaten. His head was bowed as if in prayer and his beard spread out over his chest. He was snoring softly. Robert thought he knew the man, thought his name was Roy.

"So, I didn't know you knew this fella," Erin Pound said, breezily, to Dave.

"Years and years back and back," Dave said, smiling around a beardful of food.

"Whishkey Dave ish one of the good people," Robert said. And he smiled, for the company, for the blessings of this brief time of amity.

"Say, Bob, did you hear about Lee Brown?"

Lee Brown was widely known, not just to The Outsiders, but to most of Memphis, especially Midtown Memphis, especially Union Avenue where Lee scavenged and ate and slept. It was hard to miss him. He weighed about 300 pounds, sported a full beard, usually crusted with food and the detritus of polluted air. He wore tee-shirts and jeans and big black tennis shoes. In winter sometimes he had a coat over this. Lee dropped out of high school, ran with a rough crowd, got in trouble with the law and, at age 19, almost out of despair, took to the streets, where he had lived for over 20 years. Now, he was often seen sitting at a street corner, say Union and Belvedere, or Madison and McLean, in the middle of a grass spot on the verge or median, in the middle of mid-day bustle, fast asleep, triple chin on chest.

"He ok?" Robert asked.

"Did us proud," Whiskey Dave said. Dave had a kind, generous glint in his eye. "He is now part of that cop thing. That—"

Debra looked up. She was about to finish Dave's thought but then only smiled her sweet, delicate smile.

"The Citizens Police Academy. Took the background check, did the ten-week course and now he is—whaddya wanna call it?—liaison between the community and the cops. He especially shines working with kids, apparently."

"Lee lovezz kidzz," Robert said.

"Yeah, ain't that grand?" Dave smiled, still spooning food into his face.

A pleasurable camaraderie fell over the group. Erin Pound was smiling at Robert. Her hair did those little feathery corkscrew things around her face. It was endearing and fetching. Her sweater, robin's egg blue, glowed in Robert's watery, palsied perception. She was an angel. He was convinced.

"Saw Queeg today," Dave said.

"Me too," Robert Walker said, with an acidity.

"I know. He's a shit. He said if I saw you that he had a book to show you. One you would find interesting."

"Mm," Robert said, noncommittally.

"He said you would know what it's worth. He said, and I quote, you would appreciate the points that make it a find."

Now Erin Pound was looking at Robert Walker.

"What is this, Robert," she said. "Are you bookish?"

He smiled with discomfort. "Debra," he said, pointing his fork at her. "She's the literary one in this group." It was part deflection and part acknowledgment. "What are you reading?" Robert asked.

Debra set her fork down, gently. And gently, she

bent over her bag. From within it she pulled her dog-eared Iris Murdoch paperback.

"I love Iris Murdoch!" Erin Pound said.

Debra shoved the book back into her bag as if she had been too much bared.

Robert Walker said goodbye to Erin Pound at the rear door of St. Dymphna's. She shook his hand. The sky was already empurpling.

"I hope to see you again soon," Erin Pound said. "When Dr. Death is not here." Erin's smile twinkled. Her cheeks shone like foxfire with the waning light.

"Yesh," Robert said and laughed lightly. He reluctantly let go of Erin's hand.

Whiskey Dave and Debra stood by, waiting.

"Where are you heading now, Bob?"

"Not sure," Robert Walker said.

"Now that our hunger has been assuaged I think we shall stroll down by the river. Care to join us?"

Robert hesitated. Debra's face was hid in her book. She was reading, standing up.

"The river—I, I don't know," Robert said.

Whiskey Dave, who knew something of Robert's past and was empathetic also, changed the subject.

"You wanna meet later? Have a late night at Peabody Park? Meet in the gazebo for a smoke and some literary trialogue? We can always listen to Debra talk about Dame Murdoch."

Debra smiled but turned away.

"I gesh not," Robert said. He shook Dave's hand and touched Debra lightly on the shoulder. "You be careful," he added.

Robert watched them walk away. He had no idea

why he spurned their company when he had nothing ahead of him but lonely dark.

30

ROBERT walked eastward on Central Avenue. The evening was almost cool. The breeze seemed to be coming off the clean, green lawns. Some trees had turned and some were thinking about it. There were two children playing on the sidewalk below one of the great sweeping swards. As Robert approached only one of them looked up, a pale-skinned girl with hair like a straw-colored squall. Her companion, a boy a bit older, maybe 10 or 12, kept his head down. They were working on a sidewalk mural with colored chalk.

"Hello," Robert said.

"Hi," the girl said. The boy's head popped up and shot the girl a look of warning.

"What are you drawing?" Robert asked.

There was a period of silence. The girl looked to Robert and to the boy. The boy kept his head down but his hand was still.

He looked up finally. His nose was faintly porcine. "It's the apocalypse," he said.

Robert now took a good look at their elaborate artwork. It was indeed full of fury and fire and pain. There were faces contorted with agony. There were clouds made of brimstone and pitch. There was a long fiery river full of limbs and heads and bodies split like fired shells. There were half animal, half human creatures riding what looked like vegetables but may have been spaceships. There were flaming airliners, vehicles emerging from the rectums of animals. And what strange animals they were. Like something out of Bosch, or horror comics. It was disturbing, especially from such an unlikely source. It was a very dark drawing, deep reds, black streaks, the colors of thunderclouds. It was a vision, but one of nightmare, rather than the cozier light of childish imagination.

"Jeeshush," Robert said

"Careful," the boy said, seriously. His small hand closed tighter around a stick of chalk as if it were a weapon.

"Excuse me," Robert said, fighting his slur.

"Mother says this is where we all will be soon," the girl said. She said it with such a sweet, Sunday school voice, that Robert wasn't sure he'd heard her correctly.

"I think we have shum time left," Robert said, pleasantly. "I really think we do."

The boy now shifted his position so he could look Robert in the face. His stare was noxious, a combination of bully and puppet.

"Whaddyou know, Mac?" he said.

Robert was nonplussed at this unexpected rejoinder.

"Nothing, I am sure," Robert said.

"Right," the boy pressed. "Nothing is exactly what you know. This is happening. This is our tomorrow." The little girl continued to look at Robert with a skewed but sweet smile.

"What happened to your face?" she asked

"Hooch, probably," the boy said.

"Palzee," Robert said.

"Is that like what cowboys did?" she asked.

Robert laughed which made the boy's spine stiffen. He squinted at Robert.

"You best be moving on," he said.

Robert bristled. He would have liked to take the boy to his parents for discipline but this seemed an unlikely and possibly risky move.

"Ok," Robert Walker said. "You're very good artisht."

"Thanks," the little girl said. The boy stared daggers.

Robert moved off down the sidewalk. Dark was coming on. Behind him he heard the boy say, "With justice he judges and makes war."

31

ROBERT reached the corner of Central and Cooper. He decided to stroll South on Cooper. He had always found the Cooper Young neighborhood one of the city's most convivial. There were people out in the streets. There was a feeling of community. Sometimes this made Robert feel excluded but, after that brief chat with the dodgy children, he needed activity, action, life. A shiver ran through him. Was the air nippier or did someone just walk over his grave?

As he neared the Cooper Young intersection he offered up a smile to the train trestle art which sat like a welcome sign over the gateway to the neighborhood. At night it was lit, faintly, subtly, as if a ghost family lived within.

He was drawn to Black Lodge Video. They were open till midnight and run by a pair of guys who really knew movies, especially horror films and Asian films. And they rarely threw bums out. Robert wanted to sit on their couch and watch whatever action-packed piece of the Hollywood dream they were showing on their television. As Robert climbed the hill the owner's cat Smoosh came out to meet him. He wanted to enter when Robert entered. They did together.

The fellow behind the desk, bespectacled and balding, greeted Robert the same way he might greet the mayor. It was the egalitarianism of the place that made Robert feel well and whole. Robert walked slowly up and down the walls of movies. He was attracted to the porn in the front room, if only for the brightly colored fantasy the covers offered. In the next room the movies were grouped by directors: Fellini, Godard, Bergman, Kurosawa, Frankenheimer, Altman, Bunuel, Ophuls, Lang. Robert used to watch movies. He used to love movies.

The past hit Robert Walker like a scalding needle behind his eyes, a remembrance like a migraine. He felt dizzied. He stumbled back into the front room and landed on the couch, which was uncharacteristically empty. He put his hands over his face. The palsied side sang like a flame.

Robert dozed. He jerked his head up when a group of kids caromed past him. Their laughter was free and loud and a punch to Robert's head. He was still dizzy. He didn't want to stand and risk passing out in the store's front room. The movie on the big screen TV was *Suspiria*. Its lurid colors and strange music hypnotized Robert. He tried breathing rhythmically to calm himself. The movie was pulsating.

A stab of light. A screech. And then blackness like thunder.

32

Robert Walker woke slowly. He swam upward. The face above his was friendly, blurred like an address on a dampened envelope. Robert blinked, or winked since one eye didn't open or close at will.

The face gradually crystallized into the kind contours of Whiskey Dave's.

"Dave," Robert said.

"There you go, Bob," Dave said, smiling inside his ragged beard. "Take it slow, my friend."

Robert looked around. There was a minor gathering, a coven. The Black Lodge guy stood to one side, his face concerned. Pete the Hunchback stood behind Dave, shuffling nervously from foot to foot. And, behind them all, as if trying to fade into a corner, stood Debra. She smiled a Giaconda smile when Robert's eyes found her.

"What?" Robert said.

"Blacked out," Dave said. "Like a bride at the altar."

"Wh—where?"

"You're in Black Lodge."

"Yes, I—"

"Look, there's Matt. He's the owner. You know Matt," Dave continued.

"Of coursh," Robert said.

"Robert, Robert, Robert, Rob, Rob," Pete the Hunchback said. "Gone, gone, but back, back."

"Hey, Pete," Robert said. "Hey, Debra."

Pete shuffled forward. "Looka this, Rob—Robert."

He had a new pin. White letters on a black background

said, "I am not Jim."

"True enough, Pete. Dave how did you—"

"Didn't you hear us calling you, Bob-o?" Whiskey Dave said. "You passed right by us. Peabody Park. We thought you were headed to Peabody Park to meet up with us, but you passed like the wind. We found Pete cadging outside Otherlands. Queeg was there, too, you probably don't wanna hear. Lots of outsiders about tonight. Beautiful night, right?"

Robert tried sitting up slowly. He made it with the help of Dave and Matt. His head still felt swimmy and there was pressure on his groin. A soft pressure like warmth, like numbness. Then he realized the cat was in his lap.

"Smoosh," Robert said.

"Friendsh," Robert said.

"That's it, Robert," Pete said. "Friends of yours. We're friends of yours. That a boy."

Dave smiled indulgently. He slipped a bottle into Robert's hands. Robert took a slow swallow. He shut his eyes hard like a schoolboy trying to concentrate.

"When you feel up to it you wanna go find someplace to sit and talk?"

"Yesh," Robert Walker said. He needed company. He needed other people. This felt like a revelation in the vulnerable position he found himself in. He reached out a hand to Debra. She smiled, ducked her chin into her chest. Her lovely brown hair dropped over her eyes, which fizzed like small pinwheels. Debra's eyes were like a chocolate caramel, the outer iris darker, almost to the point of being black. She almost took a step forward.

"Yeah, yeah," Pete said. "Talk. That's what you need,

buddy. Talk. We'll all just go and have a confabulation. Ain't that right? Ain't that right, Whiskey Dave?"

"Right-o, Pete. As soon as Robert can walk."

33

THE quartet made their way down Cooper, heading south into the heart of the vibrant nighttime district. On cool autumn evenings the area was teeming as if a block party had been announced. The whole neighborhood seemed to be humming, a hymn to ease and enjoyment and entertainment. And the air was redolent of frying things: the same perfume one found at the Mid-South Fair, a heady mixture of grease and mustard and beer. The sidewalks were crowded. Outside every restaurant sidewalk tables were full and conversations drifted on the breeze.

Only Pete, passing an outside diner, stuck his hand out. He got a single French fry as reward. The others were intent on finding a nice place to sit and rest. Dave appeared to enjoy the atmosphere, as if he were the equal of anyone here, as if he was harkening back to a past where he was a boulevardier himself. Robert was feeling sullen and beat-down. His face ached and he was tired and his brain was still flashing from his fainting spell, acute colored sparks behind his eyes.

Then Whiskey Dave put a hand on Robert Walker's arm, stopping him. Dave was trying to draw Robert's attention away from something. He was standing on tiptoe to make his eyes on a line with Robert's.

"Maybe best another way, eh?" Dave said.

Robert looked bewildered. He put a hand over his dead, down-weeping eye and blinked the other.

"Wh—" he asked.

"Peabody School is right round here," Dave said. "Nice playground there. Dark, private."

Then Robert saw what was making Dave behave so extraordinarily. Sitting at one of the tables on the wooden deck at Café Olé was Lyn. She wore a sleeveless beige dress and her red hair, a frizzled aura around her lovely freckled face, was catching the neon lights of the street. Her mouth, the size and color of a rosebud, was pursed in a pucker of either pleasure or perplexity. Beside her sat a man, handsome as a bourbon ad. Lyn was looking right at Robert.

Robert Walker didn't know where to put his eyes. He wanted to be far away. But he was immobile. He didn't want to see Lyn. He didn't want Lyn to see him.

Dave placed a gentle hand on Robert's bicep.

"Peabody School, Bob," he said. "A good chat, eh? Might have a little whiskey left, eh? Wanna go now?"

Pete bounced up and down.

"Aa—" Robert said. His voice choked. Lyn was making her way through the tables to the porch railing around the restaurant's deck. She wore a tight smile like the smile on a doll. As she got closer her expression changed to one of concern.

"Robert," she said, then, "Bobby" and she placed a tentative hand on the lapel of his jacket, as gentle as a moth alighting there. The railing between them was like a fence between dogs. Lyn moved her hand to Robert's cheek.

"What—what happened, dear?" she asked.

Robert didn't like the sound of "dear." He didn't like Lyn's concern. He wanted to be far away.

"Bellz palschy," Robert said. His lisp seemed even

thicker than usual, like oatmeal, like mucus.

"I've heard of that," Lyn said. "Is it serious?"

"Don't think so," Robert Walker said to his ex-wife.

"Well, how are you? Other than this, I mean. How in general are you? I've thought of you often and worried a bit, I admit."

She had said too much.

Robert looked at her. The lights of the restaurant haloed her pretty red hair.

"Ok," he said, finally.

"All right then," Lyn said. She put her hand back on Robert's coat. "I better get back. I'm with a friend."

The word stung like lye.

"Can I call you?" Lyn asked, as she shuffled backwards.

"I'll call you," Robert said and he ducked his head and moved away. His eye was tearing but he was not sure whether he was crying or not.

34

THERE was a delicate mist falling as the four outsiders moved west down Young Avenue. There were auras around the street lamps that resembled watercolor dandelion fluff. The four amblers passed the house some Cooper Youngers called Big Pink, an oversized barn that looked like a cross between a Victorian gingerbread castle and The Addams Family Home. There was a decorated iron fence between the street and the wraparound porch. The yard was trashy and the trim on the house badly in need of care but the house had presence.

They walked down a dark sidewalk that ran along Peabody School's eastern parking lot to the rear of the building where the neighborhood, in conjunction with the school, had built a playground, which included colorful jungle gyms and a sandbox, and a large, grassy area for general gamboling about, or for kickball or softball.

They sat on the damp playground equipment. Robert Walker was sunk in upon himself.

"Think this drizzle will blow over. Won't be too bad an outside night," Whiskey Dave said to no one in particular. "Won't be a bad night," he reiterated.

Debra started to bring her book out from her pocket, fingered the edge for a moment and then thought better of it. Pete couldn't sit still. He was doing a series of loping loops around the grassy infield. Despite his back he was as graceful as a dancer and the other three watched him with something like pleasure if not joy.

The mist did indeed begin to let up. A silence descended instead, just as soft, just as close to the edge of sadness.

"Where you tonight?" Whiskey Dave said, nudging Robert with an elbow.

"Don't know. Back to the park, I imagine."

"I'm gonna see Debra is safe and then I might see how the golf course looks tonight. I do like sleeping on those greens. Feels like the infield. Nice night to be outdoors now, too."

"Willy said he knew of a new subdivision where there were many unlaid sewer pipes. Sewer pipes are spacious and great place to sleep out of the weather," Debra said. It was quite a pronouncement from her.

Debra reached out and touched the sleeve of Robert's shirt with just her slim, brown fingertips. It was like the hesitant touch of a child. Robert looked at her and Debra smiled. She wanted Robert to smile, too. She looked beautiful in the semi-dark, like a burnt-sienna deity.

Now Robert let the tears flow. He put his hands over his face and sobbed.

"Here, here," Dave said. He put an arm around Robert. "Forget it, Bob. Let it go. Cry it out, Buddy."

Robert, full of shame, leaned into Whiskey Dave's embrace. He let him hold him as if he were an injured comrade in battle. And perhaps that was what he was. Perhaps Dave saw it that way.

"Lyn, right?" Whiskey Dave said, after a moment.

Pete had moved closer and was now jigging directly in front of Robert.

"Hey, hey," he said. "Hey, hey, Robert."

"Yesh," Robert said, snuffling, wiping a sleeve across his face. "That was Lyn. Should have introduced you, I guesh."

"Forget it, Bob. Forget her. Listen. You're gonna be ok. You got friends. You'll get back into it. You're not an old floater, on the ooze, like me. You'll get back in the game. There will be peace, again. There will be balance. Your ghosts will fade like fog. There will be other women. Trust me, Bob. Really."

Robert looked at Dave's weathered, whiskered face. There was warmth and kindness there like a sempiternal imprint.

"I have a lunch date tomorrow," Robert said. He didn't know why he would bring this up now. Was it a golden ring? A life preserver? No, he thought. Let it not be that.

"There you go," Dave said, softly.

"Gayla. Gayla," Robert snuffled. "What kind of a name ish that?"

"Gayla, the grad student?" Dave said.

Robert looked in his eyes.

"She looks like that actress? Blond. That actress?"

"Gwynneth Paltrow," Robert Walker said.

"Right. Right. I know her, too."

"Thatsh amazing," Robert said. He was smiling now but there was a flutter of anxiety in his chest.

"She's doing that study, right? On the homeless, for her dissertation or something?"

35

"Aw, Jaysus, Bob, I said the wrong thing, damn me. What is it, Bob? What is this Gayla to you?"

"Nothing, nothing," Robert Walker said. He stood up and walked around a bit. The others watched him in awkward silence. The moon emerged from the clouds, a good solid autumn moon. The school playground was washed in soapy light.

"I'll be going," Robert said. "Itsh late."

"Say, Doctor, listen," Whiskey Dave said. "Lemme get Debra situated and I'll come with you, what do you say?"

"It'll be ok, Dave. I'm ok."

Dave hesitated. He didn't know what to do next. Debra stood behind him. She put her hand to her cheek and brushed aside a tear.

"Hey, hey, I'll go with," Pete said. "I'll see to Robert. He'll be ok with Pete."

"How will that be, Bob? Pete'll go with you and I'll catch up to you."

"Yeah, ok," Robert said.

Whiskey Dave shook Robert's hand. He gave him a hug.

"I mean it, man. I'll catch up. Where you gonna go?"

"I'll shee you in the morning, Dave. Really. It'll be ok. Pete'll go with me. Go tuck in on the green."

"Ok, Buddy," Dave said and he and Debra moved off. They were quickly lost in tree shadow. The leaves arching over Young Avenue had something of a Washington Irving feel to them. Pete and Robert began their slow

Robert Walker

walk westwards. Pete reined in his energy in deference to Robert's mood.

After a while, as they moved Northward on McLean, Pete spoke.

"Hey, how about the river, Robert? You feeling like sleeping by the river? Always cures the sads in me. Always blows the Memphis blues away. What do you say? We find a place in Ashburn Park. Hey? Ashburn Park is a great place to sleep. Let the river enter your dreams. Dream of mermaids and angels."

"Sure," Robert Walker said.

Pete kept up a friendly patter all the way westward down Peabody, then Linden. It was a long walk but it was easing some of the poison out of Robert Walker's system. The night had turned unexpectedly beautiful. One of those lagniappe evenings of perfect weather Memphis occasionally dished up.

36

By the time they reached Riverside Drive traffic was sparse. The road was a ribbon of streetlight. Pete skipped ahead of Robert on the asphalt. It was as if the St. Vitus in him could only be held in check for so long.

Soon they were in darkness, an area of grass and tangle in the vicinity of the Memphis Arkansas Bridge. Robert thought they were near Martyrs Park and he assumed this was where Pete wanted to bed down. There were a few people about yet though the park itself closed at 8 pm. Robert saw that Pete was deep in conversation with a couple, a well-dressed man and woman who looked like they just came from a fancy dinner, some yards ahead of him. Robert hung back for the huddle looked private. Soon, Pete came skipping back to him.

"Robert, Robert," Pete said. "You know Mack, right? Mack Stile? You know him. That's him and his lady. They got a house-sitting gig. Nice house. Near here. Nice house. On Illinois. Or maybe California. Anyway. They got beds for us. Beds, Robert. Invited us to come along."

This didn't sound right to Robert. He didn't like the plan nor the appearance of the couple. He worried for Pete. Pete would follow anyone anywhere. He was so trusting, so sanguine, all day, every day.

"Naw, Pete," Robert said. "You go. I am gonna shleep here by the river. By the Rivers of Babylon." Robert tried to smile. His jaw ached. He wanted to go to sleep.

"Robert, Robert, you sure? Nice house, Robert?"

"I'm sure, Buddy. You go. Shleep well."

"Ok, ok. Come back in the morning and check on you, ok? Come back tomorrow early."

"Yesh, Pete. Thank you. I'll be fine."

And Pete skipped off into the glim under a streetlamp where the couple waited. He watched as the three went off together. Pete didn't look back. He was telling them some wild tale perhaps, or perhaps he had already forgotten Robert. Like many Outsiders Pete was mostly nocturnal.

Robert found a narrow dark spot under some trees in Martyrs Park. He looked at the odd sculpture which, in the diminishing light, seemed to be moving like the ripples of the river. Something about yellow fever victims was carved in its base. Robert tried to remember if it was near here that George Putt had killed one of his victims. The Memphis Murders, they called them, as if there were no other homicides worthy of the alliterative tag. But he shook off such thoughts. He needed to sleep. He needed respite. He needed darkness, sweet, open-handed darkness. He lay with his head cradled on his arms like a child. He wept quietly. Then, with only the moon as a nightlight, Robert wiped his tears, pressed his one dead eyelid shut, and closed his other eye on the day.

Robert fell asleep quickly. He dreamed another automobile dream, another dream where he had no steering wheel, no brakes, no control, and the road twisted and rose and then all that waited ahead was an abyss off the end of a broken ramp. Robert rolled in his sleep but he did not wake.

He did not wake till the first salmon rays of dawn began to filter through the trees. He woke because a teenage kid was peeing on him while a ratty compatriot stood nearby laughing as if he had drowned a dog.

TWO

Memphis, Tennessee, Tuesday, October 3, 2006

37

ROBERT Walker wakes. He stretches. The horrible miscreants skip off laughing into dawn's glazed mist. Now Robert Walker smells of pee. Now he is brought to full consciousness and remembers who he is, what he is, and the pain in his jaw is acute. He can't recall if he has aspirin left and if he does where he got them. His head is full of bees. He fumbles in his pocket and pulls out a packet of aspirin and he chews four of them. Now his throat burns with their salty salvation. He rises, in search of water.

Pete the Hunchback is nowhere in sight. Wherever he went he stayed. Robert hopes he is well, that his night was peaceful, his sleep without incubi, his wakening kinder than Robert's. Maybe Pete opted to get arrested. He did that often for a cot and three hot. He was well-known down at 201, that is, 201 Poplar, the lockup.

As if in recompense for the cruelty of those malicious teens Robert found an unopened can of Sprite lying underneath a clump of boxwood shrub. Probably left from someone's picnic in this wee, neat park. The can is warm but the Sprite tastes like quenched desire. This is how Robert begins his day's peregrinations, walking along the Mississippi River, drinking warm Sprite, wishing he didn't smell like what he is: a bum.

The first light of morning on the river looked like gold highlights in a beautiful woman's auburn hair. Robert knew a woman like that once. Her name was Sherri Hardwick. It was long ago. She was—she was—a castle in the air.

Then Robert found his second treasure of the early day: at his feet, shining like a fairy-tale charm, glinting with dawn light as if only to catch his eye, was a small silver button. Robert bent and picked it up and recognized, on a nail-polish red background, the logo from Woodstock: "3 Days of Peace and Music." Pete would love it.

Robert Walker walked north toward Mud Island and humanity.

Two deprivations assailed him. He needed breakfast and he needed to move his bowels. And, as if his lower plumbing were attached to his heart, he then recalled the sadness that sent him to sleep last night, the betrayal of Gayla Calley, the appearance of Lyn on the arm of a handsome knight-errant.

Yet he knows that Gayla Calley did not betray him. It was only his foolish heart, his moony mind, which made her into something more than an investigator, a mad scientist in life's sad laboratory.

Robert passed The Orpheum, now a quiet shell. He was seeking an eastbound avenue with fast food restaurants. There he would find a handout perhaps. There a bathroom.

At Union Robert headed back East. He thought there was someplace near AutoZone Park but once he got there it was all quiet as if it were a holiday. Then he realized it was very early in the day and the commuters hadn't even started for work. Downtown can be quiet during its off hours, like a buried city.

He stopped at an Exxon Mart and leaned against the walls near the bathroom. His head hurt and his eye stung. There were few patrons. An old black gentleman, bent over his cane, hobbled past Robert and into the restroom. When he came back out Robert gave him a curtailed smile, his half Sardonicus grimace. The fellow stopped and fixed Robert with his own yellow eye.

Robert was suddenly a little afraid and, inwardly, he shrank back. But the old man was moving his hand around in his shabby pocket and after a protracted moment he pulled out a quarter. He smiled a snaggle-toothed grin and dropped it into Robert's hand, which Robert had extended by reflex. Robert now tried a better smile. He started to speak, to tell the old guy thanks anyway, but the gentleman had already turned away. He shuffled back toward his car, a rusted Oldsmobile on shot shocks. Inside was a woman as old as the man and, in the back seat, a beautiful girl child who waved to Robert with her hand clad in a little white Sunday school glove.

Some folks went by him as if he were invisible.

A teenager called him a parasite.

One man, who looked like a priest on his day off, tried to engage Robert in a debate. Robert was not in the mood. He tried to dismiss the stubborn fellow.

"Nobody ish gonna make you give," Robert said.

"True enough," the clean-cut citizen said as if he had just scored a point.

"Jesus said you should always give." Robert felt his gorge rise. His pain, his wretchedness meant nothing to strangers. He knew that as well as he knew his own name.

"Yeah, Tolstoy said that, too," the man said and tipping an imaginary hat, moved on.

Eventually, Robert was able to wheedle a few dollars more. It was enough for food, for coffee. He went into the gas station's market and spent a few moments standing stock still in front of racks of snacks, trying to concentrate. He wanted breakfast food but the pickings were slim. There were salty Brim snacks, generic donuts the size of Tonka truck tires, generic candies with strange consistencies, like worms, or barely chewable plastic. He had to have something. He felt sad and alone and he wanted to wake up and try to salvage the day. Haphazardly he chose a Rice Krispies bar and at the counter the largest coffee offered. He put enough sugar into the coffee that it thickened, like gravy. He remembered to grab a straw. The clerk gave him a look the Apostle Thomas would have envied.

Outside Robert Walker found a curb to the western side of the station, a sad plot of ragged grass and dirt and human accrual surrounded by concrete. He couldn't imagine that this piece of inner-city landscaping pleased anyone. He sucked some coffee through the straw and managed to not dribble into his beard. The Rice Krispies bar tasted of sugar and chemicals. He ate it swiftly, as if he were ashamed, and washed it down with large guzzles of coffee. One of the better advancements of the 21st century, Robert thought, not for the first time, was that good coffee was everywhere. Or perhaps it only tasted good in comparison to the overly sweet candy.

In the bathroom Robert moved his bowels and then washed his face and hands in front of the murky mirror. He assessed his spoiled face. With one reddened, droopy eye that didn't blink, as if it were glass, and a corner of his mouth downturned and spittle in his grey-flecked beard, Robert thought he looked like the butt end of nothing. He looked like Popeye's Pappy. He looked like death, old death. He tried wiping down his urine-marked jacket with some rough paper towels. He should have gone back inside for some baby wipes or something that might swab away the odor but he wasn't sure he had enough money and he didn't want to face that clerk again.

Robert Walker headed eastward down Union Avenue. He needed companionship perhaps. He needed to blow the blues away.

38

Now the traffic heading west on Union was heavy and the noise and the dirty air swirled around Robert like a casual eddy of desolation. He was trying hard not to think. He would not think of Lyn. He would not think of this Gayla Calley and her project. Robert did not want to be anyone's project. He would not meet her at lunch. She could sit in The Cupboard with her meat and three by herself. Robert never wanted to be studied.

As Robert walked he noticed the almost complete absence of his Outsider friends. Was there something going on that he was unaware of? A police sweep? A movement against vagrancy? He had heard there had been some trouble downtown. Good, solid citizens were tired of bums looking for handouts. "They're so aggressive," one woman told a reporter for The Commercial Appeal.

As Robert approached the Starbucks at Union and McLean he found himself suddenly craving another coffee, a syrupy coffee thickened by heavy whipped cream, a latte full of calories and sweet heat. He grubbed around in his pocket to see what he had left. Change. No bills. He realized he hadn't begged enough for the day. Robert Walker was not proud of being a spare change artist. His begging had specific aims, to buy a meal or two. He was a beggar of the moment and rarely carried money with him. It was too easy to get rolled by other bums or youngsters like those two monsters in the park this morning. But, now Robert didn't feel like asking anyone for help. His sadness spread into his furious ear and into his chest and arms. He felt heavy, tired as if he had lived too long. He sat on the wall next to Las Savell's Jewelers. The cars rushing by were an abrasive music. Was it possible that the palsy made his ears more sensitive? He had no idea. This outer space malady was new to him, this curse, this ravaging.

Robert sat still and hung his head. He manually closed his bad eye. A tear leaked out of the corner of his good eye and the realization reached Robert's brain that his bad eye wasn't blinking, and, if it weren't blinking it was most likely drying out. And with this thought the eye sparked as if he had tapped it with a hot match.

39

Robert begged enough extra change for a thick, sugary and hot latte. A fellow in full running regalia actually stopped and gave him a few bucks, pulling bills from an ingenious blue packet at his waist, as he stood there panting and huffing. He was handsome and thin as an exclamation mark. Runners rarely stopped.

The day was not overly cool for this time of year in Memphis but sleeping down by the river had let a chill into his bones. Robert Walker felt heavy cold, as if he had picked up a coat of rime. The young woman behind the counter at Starbucks wrinkled up her nose as Robert approached. It was a subtle gesture. Perhaps she was unaware of doing it. Robert had made a personal study of such gestures, the small physical movements people use to separate themselves from such symbols of loss and diminishment as street people, as if they were afraid failure would rub off on them. Or perhaps it was simple revulsion.

Cupped in both hands the coffee felt like a holy rite when he finally raised it to his lips. Latte ran from the dead corner of his mouth. Robert was too self-conscious to get a straw. He fumbled his last three aspirin into his mouth and swallowed. He continued to sip slowly, still standing by the sweetener display.

From his peripheral vision he picked up someone's gawk. He lowered the cup and focused his eyes on the tables and chairs. The usual laptop writers and university students were there in their bright fall colors. Lonely poets. Lovers. But right in the middle of the group sat Queeg, a malicious grin on his face. He stood out like a canker. It was always thus with Queeg. He intimidated by behaving as if he knew something you should know. Robert started to turn and Queeg called out.

"Walker, man, Walker, get your ass over here," Queeg said in a loud, hearty voice. His face gleamed with a garden of gin blossoms and rosacea.

40

Robert reluctantly sat at Queeg's table. Robert held the steaming coffee close to his face. It soothed him.

"Man, your face looks like shit," Queeg said in mock friendly tones.

Robert held his peace. He concentrated on keeping the coffee from running out of the side of his mouth.

"How are you?" Queeg continued to press. His grin was like the soldier's sword cut in Christ's side.

"What do you want?" Robert finally spoke.

"Nothing, man, nothing. A little camaraderie. A little huddle. Book talk. You wanna talk books?"

Robert shook his head. He kept the coffee cup near his mouth as if it were a mask.

"You can help me. You gotta help me. We can make some money with this."

Robert knew better than to get involved with Queeg, especially with any business plans.

Queeg reached down to the ground and pulled up a ratty satchel. It was the kind businessmen used for travel a long time ago. It was beaten and scratched and the latch on it was held together with a piece of wire. Reaching in Queeg pulled out a bulky rectangular package, wrapped in a tie-dye scarf.

"This is it, my friend," John "Queeg" George said. The package smelled like Queeg himself, a dishonest smell like an old warehouse. "This is the Holy Grail."

Robert's curiosity was piqued but he resisted the pull.

"I have to go," Robert said.

Queeg put a hand on Robert's arm. Coffee sloshed onto Robert's already stained sweatshirt.

"Sit down," Queeg said. His voice whistled like a rat's.

"Goddamit," Robert Walker said. "Goddamit, Queeg."

"Ok, ok, sorry," Queeg said now, all mollification. "Sit. Please."

Robert wavered, half standing. Then he resettled himself.

"What ishit?" he said.

Anger again flashed across Queeg's ruby face. "It's not shit, Brother," he seethed.

"What izz it?" Robert hit his words hard.

"Oh, right. Sorry. Here."

He handed the package to Robert. Robert put his coffee down and began to slip the scarf off the book. Inside the scarf it was also wrapped in thin foam packing material. His hands knew what it was even before his brain knew.

It was a Limited Editions Club copy of Joyce's Ulysses, the one with the 20 Matisse lithograph drawings, the one signed by Matisse. Brown, cloth-covered boards, with an exquisite Matisse design in gold, matching the gold embossing on the spine. Limited edition of 1500 copies. Worth a healthy chunk of change. Rare. And rarer still in this condition which was near pristine.

"Wow," Robert couldn't help but say. "Extraordinary."

"Rare as a John Calipari fan in Massachusetts."

"Huh."

"Right, right, I told you. We can do it. Whaddya think? We sell this. We split the profits."

Robert was moved. He felt an old itch begin again

as if from a thousand years ago. It wasn't the money. It was the honor of the book. The integrity. He wanted to be connected to this book, to have it briefly and to see it sent along on its journey. This appealed to Robert, even in the state he was in. This inspired him like nothing had in a while. He ran his hands along the cloth. He gently put his cleanest finger on the spot where the great Matisse laid his pen. He put his nose to the book's gutter and breathed in its essence.

"It's worth $5000 easy. In this condition maybe 6 or 7. Easy. But I know a guy, a rich East Memphis collector who is a Joyce nut. He'd give us 10 grand without blinking. Maybe more. How about it? 5 or 6 grand each. Huh?"

Queeg was practically salivating.

Robert looked at the book. He looked at Queeg. And then he understood why Queeg was making such an offer. The book was hot. He stole it and Robert knew from where. There was a Limited Editions Club collection in a temperature controlled room in the Rhodes College library, a donation from the late Walter Armstrong. How Queeg managed such a heist Robert could not fathom. Queeg had no scruples and Robert was sure that this collector wouldn't deal with a scoundrel like Queeg. Queeg believed Robert would make a better salesman than himself. This was the only reason Queeg was foisting this on him.

Robert fixed Queeg with his one good eye. His head ached. His ear flamed.

"Fuck," Robert Walker said. "Fuck, Queeg. You shtole this. No, Goddamit. I will not be party to this."

Robert rose and reached for his coffee. Queeg's

hand closed on it faster. And just as fast he threw the remaining coffee in Robert's face. It was only slightly hot.

Robert clenched his fists. He had never struck another human being. His heart beat a ragged tattoo. He could not speak. He could barely breathe. Then, suddenly, he remembered where he was. The entire Starbuck's crowd was looking at him.

Meanwhile, Queeg was furiously wiping off a drop of coffee which landed on the chipped glassine wrapper of the Ulysses. Queeg glanced once around him, grabbed book and bag and hustled out, bumping patrons, hitting tables with his hip.

Robert collected his wits for a moment.

A young college student at one of the tables came over to him.

"You ok, sir?" the boy asked.

Robert looked at him. He was sincere. He was young like white paper yet unmarked.

"Yesh," Robert said. "Thank you."

41

OUTSIDE Starbucks Robert Walker assessed the day. He was angry and tired. He could head east out Union, toward the library's main branch, where he occasionally went. He went there on days when it didn't hurt to think about books. Sometimes he even sat inside and read. The library didn't love the homeless but neither did they seem particularly paranoid concerning them. Or he could go south down McLean, back toward the Cooper-Young neighborhood, where there was some sort of acceptance, some sort of goodwill. He could even head north down McLean.

Once Robert had walked to Raleigh, which sat like Northern moss on the side of the tree of the larger city. One of his childhood friends, whom he met in Cub Scouts, still lived in Raleigh. Robert used to visit him and the two of them spent many pleasant hours on Stage Road, which, back then, was two lanes wide. On Stage Road, at the intersection with Jackson Avenue, there was Raleigh Drug Store, where once Robert and this childhood friend, Gary, saw a Duncan yo-yo expert put on a show. They had also gotten vanilla cokes from the counter. On Stage Road, also, was a mystic little emporium called The Hobby Shop. Partly a place to take art lessons (Gary was a very fine draughtsman and drew pictures of Raleigh homes and businesses where those works of art still hang) and partly a child's paradise, where one could buy Revell model kits, Green Lantern or Fantastic Four comic books, matchbox cars, India rubber balls, magic tricks, Mad Magazine, exploding cigarette loads, little green army men, chess sets, chewing gum packages with a small mousetrap-like snapper inside, invisible ink, plastic Ratfinks, baseball cards, and Chinese handcuffs.

Once, earlier this year, before the summer heat socked in, Robert had walked to Raleigh. It took him the better part of three hours. He found the house where he thought his friend Gary had lived. He knocked on the door. A gentle drizzle was falling. There was a new Buick in the driveway. Robert rang the bell. He thought he heard movement inside and he thought he saw the living room curtain moved aside and quickly dropped back into place. Robert stood on his friend's porch that day and realized something dolorous, something that was both a relief and a malignance. He didn't want to talk to Gary either. Robert walked back to Memphis.

42

I⊤ wasn't that memory of Raleigh which kept Robert Walker in Midtown this day. What he needed was to walk around in the sunshine and hope it burned off the piss and coffee from his habiliments. He wanted to return to St. Dymphna's for a shower and fresh clothes but he didn't know if there were rules about how often one could make use of their compassionate services. Whiskey Dave would know but Robert didn't know how to find Whiskey Dave. Erin. Robert now began to think of Erin, her kindness, her angelic face. This only made him bluer.

Robert walked east. The businesses were opening. Cars were speeding past, mostly going downtown. He wondered, not for the first time, what all these people did downtown. Bankers, lawyers, traders. People who, when asked what they did for a living would answer, with a near orphic grin, "Futures." As if there was more than one. And perhaps there will be.

Robert didn't understand today any better than he had ever understood. There were a lot of people making money somehow. Just look at the homes along the Parkway, along Belvedere, in Hein Park and Central Gardens and East Memphis. Homes big enough for four families each. Again he pondered: was there really that much money to be made? Was it easy, that so many people were able to achieve it? Robert Walker didn't know before he was one of the Outsiders and he sure didn't know now.

Robert Walker

He walked on.

At the corner of Union and Parkway Robert wandered onto the grassy courtyard of the Memphis Theological Seminary. This was one of the prettiest buildings in Memphis and its grounds were spacious, landscaped and hospitable. Robert sat on a small stone wall which ran along its front sidewalk. The sun felt good on his face. His clothing was drying stiff and incrusted, mucky like a bad science experiment. Two well-dressed, princely men were coming up the sidewalk toward him. From a distance their recognition of him seemed a bad portent. Surely, these are men of God, Robert thought. They had to be charitable.

As they drew closer Robert gave them a lopsided smile. They didn't *not* return the smile. Their grins were strained, curious, perhaps even offended. Robert wanted to follow them inside. He wanted to walk halls that he imagined were dim and redolent of old dark wood and polished floors and a thousand years of students, passing through on their way to a religious calling. He imagined the consolation of the quiet and dusky interior to the building. Robert Walker wanted inside. He imagined it so thoroughly that it made him ache. He wanted to feel dry and safe. He wanted inside.

Instead, he slowly rose and walked further east on Union.

As the sun climbed the sky Robert began to wonder about lunch. He was tired of begging. He was tired of standing outside service stations and fast food restaurants. He was tired of the begrudged coin, the shaming stares.

He wanted to find Whiskey Dave and Pete the

Hunchback. They would listen to his story about Queeg and the impossibly valuable book and the violent confrontation. They would commiserate about getting pissed on down by the river. Pete, poor Pete, had suffered much worse. Perhaps Dave would be at Java Cabana, a Cooper-Young coffeehouse. Mary, who ran it, knew Dave and normally stood him to a cup of coffee and a roll. Mary, who was sexy like the actress Carla Gugino, was kind to Robert, as well. She was kind to all friends of Dave's because there was something in their pasts that bonded them. Robert was not sure what it was but it didn't matter. Mary was good people.

So, Robert doubled back and headed south down Parkway. The mansions on either side of the six-lane divided road, where monsters flew by in their shadowy vehicles, stood like massifs, carved from living rock by eons of weather. Robert hated the Parkway. Not because he was reminded of how far down he had slid in society's pecking order, but because it buzzed, dirty and loud and half-lit, as if the air, full of exhaust and detritus and dust, were filtered through a sullied curtain.

Robert Walker passed the Kwik-Shop and Deli (which made his mouth water) and Memphis Animal Clinic at the corner of Parkway and Central. And then the weedy, derelict area where once The Memphis Fairgrounds and Mid-South Fair held their annual gala exhibition and raree show, with its noise and music and men and horses' hoops and garters and hogsheads of real fire. No more, no more. The fair had moved on. The antique wooden roller coaster, the one Elvis was partial to, any Memphian would tell you, was dismantled and sold. The area now looked as bleak as the surface of the moon.

43

WALKING west up Young Avenue Robert was aware of a sea-change in the surrounding community. This end of the Cooper-Young neighborhood was still waiting for the renovations that had improved much of the environs before the housing market started to crater. Still, these streets, known for their crack houses and domestic disputes, had a sheen to them, an expectancy that sat on them like icing. And the new condominiums, though still mostly vacant, reflected the citrus light and made Robert's heart swell, slightly. His funk was deep, however. His abandonment still heavy inside him.

Java Cabana was open and at its one outside table sat a striking young man and his equally attractive woman. They were dressed like gypsies but Robert didn't think they were gypsies. More likely a musician and his hip infatuate. He had the lean face and sharp goatee of a jazz player, or a seasoned rocker. Robert imagined that he recognized him.

The couple nodded to Robert. Robert offered back his half smile, like an interrupted cut in a melon.

Mary was not behind the counter. Instead there sat the gorgeous black female singer who wore her wild hair Rastafarian style. Her face was the face of a Botticelli's angel, if Botticelli had painted in Harlem. A single brown mole sat on her cheek like an island in the middle of the Mississippi. She was that color, too, a rich, dark color that made Robert swoon with buried desire. She smiled.

Robert was temporarily tongue-tied.

She stared at him expectantly.

"Mary," he finally said.

"Not in yet," she said, her voice a potent blend of Caribbean and Southern twang.

"I'll just shit," Robert said, gesturing obscurely behind him at the ramshackle, varied furnishings.

"Pardon," she said.

"Shorry," Robert said and he blushed like a child. "I'll just find a...sh-eet."

But the woman had already lost interest. She was reading a *Rolling Stone*. Robert wanted to know what she was reading but instead he slunk toward a couch against the wall and dropped onto it. In the drowsy morning sunlight coming through the window Robert felt like a cat. And a cat nap was calling him from the sleepy depths. There was music playing softly. Aretha Franklin perhaps. Or Carla Thomas. Robert's head dipped onto his chest.

When he woke Mary had replaced the lovely black woman behind the counter. Robert felt stiff and chowder-headed. He was embarrassed that he had drooled into his beard and that one of his eyes was only half-closed. He stood up slowly.

When he reached the counter Mary looked up from what she was doing. She was writing a poem on a laptop computer. Robert felt as if he were intruding on something intimate.

"Hello, Robert," Mary said, looking up. Her smile held warmth the way a cup of coffee does.

"Mary," Robert said. "I didn't know that you would remember me."

"You're Dave's friend, right?"

"Yesh," Robert said.

Mary now scrutinized Robert's face. She closed her laptop.

"Anything wrong?" She asked.

"No, no," Robert said, but his hand had already risen halfway to his cheek. "I'm looking for Dave actually."

"Haven't seen him," Mary said. "Maybe Val has. Want me to get her? She's just outside having a cup and a smoke."

"No," Robert said though he didn't know why not.

"Need a cup?" Mary said, already moving toward the cappuccino machine.

"Yesh," Robert said. And then foolishly, "I haven't any money right now."

Mary just smiled and set a hot latte on the counter. Robert perched himself on one of the stools and put his hands around the cup. Mary opened her laptop again.

She hummed as she typed. The sun coming in a window made highlights in her auburn hair and she appeared a wood spirit. Robert thought she was the representation of attractive womanhood. Earth Mother. Woman Incarnate.

He sipped. Again he was revived by thick, hot decoction.

"Shkool work?" he asked, since he was feeling almost human.

Mary looked out of the corner of her eyes. Robert's ex-wife used to say, "Don't cut your eyes at me," and it became a family joke, part of their personal argot. He almost said it aloud now but stopped himself.

"Poem," Mary said. "Rotten poem."

"Why rotten?"

"Ill-conceived."

"May I read it?"

Mary now turned her full face toward Robert. "You're a funny bird, Robert. Are you a reader? A writer?"

Robert wanted to hide. This started to open him up like a surgery. He took too large a mouthful of coffee and had to let some out into his whiskers before he choked. Drinking was difficult. He had forgotten to be careful.

"No," Robert said. "That ish, I once, well..."

"You don't read anymore?" Mary asked, her voice a honeyed kindness.

"No, no," Robert said. He moved awkwardly backward off the stool.

"Robert, stop," Mary said. "Did I say something wrong?"

"No," Robert said. "Gotta go."

Mary came around the counter. She took the crook of his arm and led him to a couch. Together they sat. Robert Walker tried to make himself smaller. He wanted to twist into the fetal position.

44

MARY held Robert's hand. Mary's hand felt like kindliness, succor.

No customers disturbed them. The silence felt churchly. Eventually, Robert raised his head and looked into Mary's eyes.

"I love booksh," Robert Walker said. And he began to cry.

Mary let her silence comfort. She held his hand in one palm and patted the top of it with her other hand.

"I haven't read," Robert Walker said.

Silence again, a still, attenuated silence.

"For a long time," Robert said. "I forgot."

"What did you forget, Robert?" Mary asked.

"Reading."

"Mm. It's a soul thing, isn't it? Books. A soul thing."

"Yesh," Robert said. He wiped some mucus from the side of his nose with his jacket sleeve.

"I have some books here. Look," Mary leaned across Robert and plucked from a rickety little stand, a dog-eared paperback of Pynchon's *V.*

Robert took the book in his hand. Mary let go of his other and Robert held the book with both hands as if he were trying to warm it.

"Have you read that one?" Mary asked.

"Yesh," Robert said. "Pynchon."

Robert said the author's name as if it were a talisman, as if it held import for him, perhaps for everyone. "Pynchon," he said, again, and snuffled a few tears back.

"I have others. Would you like to take something with you?"

Robert looked the small rack over. He saw a lot of old friends.

"Always meant to read Wallace Shtegner," Robert said.

Mary leaned across Robert again. She smelled like fresh coconut. The press of her soft flesh on him almost made Robert cry again. She finally found the book he was referring to, a mass market copy of *All the Little Live Things*.

"Take it, please," Mary said.

"Thank you," Robert Walker said. "I—I better go."

"Ok," Mary said. She squeezed his hand one more time.

Outside in the dazzling sunshine Robert blinked a few times. He felt as if he had returned from a darkened cave, returned from the land of sleep into the light of day. The black soul singer was gone from the sidewalk table and instead there sat a couple of young people festooned with colorful tattoos and piercings. There was a lot of metal on their faces. Between them it must have been a pound or so. They smiled at Robert. Robert wiped the side of his bad eye with his finger in case a tear lingered there. He felt a little better.

"Wallace Shtegner," he said to the young people.

45

Heading toward mid-morning Robert walked west along Young Avenue. Goner Records didn't open until noon so Robert stood outside their window and read the hand-printed notices for local bands. Memphis music was an undying phenomenon. Robert used to love music.

Now, his face ached and his right eye was drying and stinging. He wished he had asked Mary for some aspirin. He tried holding the lid of his eye down for relief. He tried manually operating it, making it blink, hoping that would stir his tear ducts. He walked on.

At the corner of Cooper and Young Robert sat in the gazebo and pondered what to do with the rest of the day. He should find Whiskey Dave or Pete the Hunchback and see if they wanted to check dumpsters for food and have a picnic lunch in the park. Returning to Overton Park felt like the right thing to do. He was reminded of the Eliot line about returning to the beginning and knowing the place for the first time. Underneath his bushes there was some cardboard, an old shirt, a water bottle, perhaps some old candy. Right now it felt like a home to Robert and he longed to return home. The word echoed in Robert's head. He knew the antonym at work within him. Homeless. Robert Walker was homeless.

Before sadness overwhelmed him he rose and began walking down Cooper. Once again he wished for new clothes. Perhaps he should return to the park for that old shirt. It wasn't much cleaner than the one he was wearing but it did not smell of pee.

46

BECAUSE by moving he felt safer, Robert Walker moved. He walked down Young Avenue, past Café Ole where he had seen Lyn last night. It already seemed like years ago. Lyn. She is so beautiful. And she seemed happy. Past Young Avenue Deli where once he and Lyn had seen The Handsome Family perform live.

Robert passed the house called Big Pink again, then the elementary school with its encouraging sign out front. Every week the sign boasted some new parent event, some new student test, a book fair, an auction, notes to the world from the closed society that is a school, messages of aspiration. No one on the outside can quite understand. Memory dictates how we feel about it and memory lies. The past is a different country, as someone said. Robert looked up at the windows garlanded with multi-colored construction paper. Some things never change. Little clotheslines of art and science projects, hung to show progress, hung for those special parent events.

Some kids were in one of the upper windows. Two black boys in matching white shirts. They watched Robert for a while and just as he was raising his arm to salute them one of the boys flipped Robert off. They both crumbled back into the room. Robert imagined he could hear their laughter even on the street.

Further down Young it was all funky houses. The Halloween House on the corner of Young and Tanglewood was already gearing up for its once-a-year glory. The owner built a veritable haunted house on his lawn every year and drew kids from all over Midtown Memphis. Further still, there were well-kept, precision-cut lawns, that looked like stage sets from *Splendor in the Grass*, abutting lawns of dirt and rocks. Houses where uptight older folks lived next door to hippies whose idea of a garden was a plinth upon which sat a concrete frog, a hanging lantern with Christmas lights strung into it from the rotting porch, a sundial, white rocks and cypress knees. And hanging over that hippie house a tree as big as Ygdrasil, an oak from the 1800s, an oak which had probably seen the mustering of confederate troops. Robert liked this house. He could live in this house.

There was a burly guy on the sidewalk blowing leaves from his yard into the street where they would clog up the gutters and become the city's problem.

Robert nodded and said, "How are you?"

"You see this?" the guy said.

Robert looked.

"I'm blowing leaves but the guy living next door has the trees. You see?"

Robert looked. He nodded again.

"Is that fair?"

"I don't know," Robert said.

"You don't know. His trees, my work. Figure it out."

Robert kept walking.

Where Young met McLean Robert headed north. He had the vague idea that he would find Dave on Union. Up McLean, across Central, the houses were tonier, the lawns as large as playing fields, the cars fancier, the security systems expensive.

At the corner of Peabody and McLean Robert sat. He was thirsty. Coffee was not the right thing to have had without water, too. His head beat like an experimental jazz band. Up ahead was a Walgreens, a Rite-Aid, a CVS. It was pharmacy corner. Robert thought he would beg some coins and get a bottled water.

He stopped outside Walgreens and as he turned he was faced with a man as tall as a steeple. He was the biggest man Robert had ever stood next to. Perhaps he played for the University of Memphis or the Grizzlies. Everything about him was on a different scale, his arms, his chest, even his hair. His tennis shoes looked as if they were designed for astronauts, and they were the size of skateboards. Robert stepped backwards involuntarily.

"Here, brother," the giant said. He handed Robert $20.

Robert was speechless. He nodded. He put a hand to his sagging cheek.

The fellow nodded back and Robert mustered his voice and called after him. "You play ball?"

The giant turned around and smiled a smile as wide as hope.

He waved.

Robert bought 2 bottles of water, a Snickers bar, some Cheetos. When he paid with the 20 he thought the clerk looked at him funny. Perhaps not. She probably saw so much during a standard weekday that his slovenliness and unexpected bill didn't even rate.

Outside Robert drank the first bottle standing still on the sidewalk. He then moved to a small grassy area near the entrance to the parking lot, on the edge of McLean Avenue. He sat and ate the bag of Cheetos, concentrating on each one, its burst of pure flavor was almost intoxicating. Robert savored his Cheetos. Afterward he noticed that there were black clouds gathering. Soon he was going to have to find someplace with a roof. But first, he would enjoy his Snickers. And after that Robert downed the other bottle of water.

It wasn't until he stood, wiping his mouth with his sleeve that he realized he should have gotten some aspirin. He didn't want to go back into Walgreens so he went to the Rite-Aid just west on Union. There he bought a whole bottle of aspirin, two more bottles of water, and a sweet roll. Outside he took some aspirin and put the rest of his purchases in his pockets.

It wasn't until he was walking west on Union that he realized he had only eaten crap that morning. Not that he could afford to be picky but too much junk food spelled trouble when you were on your own. Getting sick became more problematic for Outsiders. Robert saw it a lot with the topers. He couldn't understand their indifference to throwing up in public. Many of them were like Pete, nocturnal. And Dave managed to drink and not make a mess of his days. Dave was one in a million.

And with these thoughts Robert remembered that he had a hot lunch waiting for him. All he had to do was show up at the Cupboard and Gayla would buy him a meat and three. And those rolls, those corn muffins. Though Robert, foolishly, felt betrayed by Gayla, he thought he should keep the appointment. His heart tried to engage but Robert transferred his concentration to his gut which was rolling now like the Mississippi itself.

47

Robert was very early so he found a quiet place in the rear of the Cupboard parking lot and there he sat down. He wanted to read his book, but he was afraid his concentration was shot. He wished for his old mind back, the one geared toward reading, the one that connected. But that was also the mind filled with spring traps, with the power of dreadful introspection. Still, for right now, he wished he could read while he waited. He wished this for the first time in months. He envied Debra's reading discipline.

What Robert didn't need was a dose of Willy's gibberish. Yet there Willy was, approaching on Robert's left, bearing down on him like a Pentecostal.

"Cap'n, Cap'n," Willy half-sobbed, skipping closer. His beard was caked with something yellow. "Cap'n, so glad to find you. Got news."

"Hey, Willy," Robert said, sadly.

"Pete, Cap'n. Gotta love Pete, right?"

Robert looked at Willy's foolish expression with impatience.

"Pete, he, Pete," Willy said. He lost his thread. He pulled at his matted beard. He began again along a different route.

"Captain, my Captain. Gotta believe, am I right? Lambs, lambs of God, lambs for dinner, for the slaughter. Lambs for the laughter. Mary, Sweet Mary, had a lamb. Mary, Mother of God, had a lamb..."

Willy stopped like a run-down gramophone. He pulled

Robert Walker

at his beard some more. And then he wandered away, off toward downtown. A block ahead Robert watched as Willy accosted a small group of young black men. Suddenly Willy was in the middle of them. Robert feared momentarily for Willy's safety but they all moved on, the young black men laughing and shaking their heads.

Robert wanted to do something, something... constructive...before lunch. He wanted to not waste time.

Instead Robert popped a few more aspirin and then lowered his head. He slept.

He woke with a start. Someone was softly speaking his name. He opened his eyes to see an angel standing over him, the sun making her blond hair an aureole of holy light. For a moment Robert did not know where he was or who this apparition could be.

"Robert," the angel spoke again. "It's Gayla. I'm so happy you made it."

Robert was embarrassed to have been found in this way, asleep with head on chest, drooling into his dirty beard, like any common bum. Robert was a common bum.

He struggled to his feet.

"Shorry," he said.

He was a bit unsteady and Gayla put a hand to his arm to steady him. After a moment she spoke again.

"Are you hungry?" she asked, smiling that Gwyneth Paltrow smile.

Robert flashed angry for a second. He wanted to say, I am a derelict. Of course I am hungry. I am a bum.

Instead he said, "Sure. Yesh."

They went inside the cozy restaurant. Robert had eaten at The Cupboard once before, years ago, with

Lyn. That night Lyn had been sad because her brother, who was a junkie, had been institutionalized one more time. They ate to distract her but it did not work. Robert remembers her pushing the food around on her plate like a child trying to hide a lack of appetite.

No one at the restaurant seemed nonplussed at Robert's appearance. They were, however seated at a booth in the rear, near the kitchen. Gayla smiled sweetly at the hostess who served them and handed them menus.

"Two sweet teas?" Gayla said to both Robert and the hostess and when Robert nodded the hostess hurried off.

Robert felt like apologizing for his smell. He imagined the urine was ripe enough to repel, to put them off their food. Instead he kept mum. He remembered that he was only an object of study for this lovely young woman, so eager to make her way, so eager to help the world while making her way.

The menu swam before Robert's eyes, even his good one. It had been a long time since he had this much choice in victuals. He knew the old meat and three was the direction he was heading but he wanted to read every word. He drank some tea and it tasted like amrita. Some of it dribbled into his beard. Gayla handed him a straw. She was smiling like Gwyneth Paltrow.

"Anything you want," she said, as if Robert had asked.

He pretended that he was concentrating so hard that he didn't hear her or notice the proffered straw. Gayla laid the straw on the tabletop between them.

When the waitress returned with a basket of rolls and cornbread, Gayla ordered a salad (naturally, thought Robert) and Robert ordered chicken fried steak with mashed potatoes, fried okra and green beans. After she left Robert buttered a cornbread muffin. He ate it in small bites. Gayla sat there grinning at him as if he were the brown-eyed handsome man.

"So, Robert," she finally said. "Tell me more. Tell me how your life is."

Robert squinted at her, a one-eyed squint.

"I'm fine," he said.

"Good," Gayla said, as if she believed him.

"Fine," he repeated as if he had gained the upper hand or something.

"Lemme tell you what I am doing," she said next. Robert put down the butter knife, the one he was preparing to use to butter another piece of cornbread. What was she going to tell him?

"I am working on my dissertation and I think you can help me."

Robert kept his counsel.

"I am particularly interested in homelessness, but not just the economic or even societal whys of it. I am most particularly interested in the intellectual side."

"Intellectual," Robert parroted. He wasn't following her.

"Yes, intellectual. What do smart people who are forced to live on the streets think, about their own situation, about the world around them, about where they came from and how they got here, and about what I like to call the relative ponderables."

"I'm not forshed to live on the street," Robert said, slurring worse around some half-masticated bread.

"I'm sorry, of course."

"Relative ponderables?"

"Yes, the things we all ask ourselves. Who am I? What does the I mean? What is my purpose and what are other people's purposes? What is love? What is death? I am interested in men and women who were once better off, intellectually, than most people and are now living on the fringes. How does that change the big questions? The relative ponderables."

Gayla's smile had grown warmer with her earnestness. Robert liked her better suddenly.

He suppressed a laugh and let it become a short cough.

"What?" Gayla said. "You have a nice smile, Robert."

"Don't—don't shay that," Robert said, but he kept a half-smile on his face. "I am laughing at myshelf. I am laughing at the folly and vanity of man."

"Ok, then."

"I am laughing because when I first saw you yesterday you shtopped my heart. I was ash we used to shay, shmitten."

"Why Robert, how nice."

"Wait," Robert said, holding up a hand. "It'sh not nice. I imagined, from shomeplace deep in my walled-over heart—nothing. Forget it. It wash a fleeting feeling of well-being but the heart yearns for such. Apparently. Foolish, foolish man."

Gayla looked at Robert hard. Her face was inscrutable.

"I am highly flattered, Robert," she said. "I have a boyfriend..."

"Itsh ok," Robert said. "You don't have to shoffen any blow. I am ok."

"Ok," Gayla said, as the waitress set their lunches before them.

48

ROBERT began to eat his food slowly. The meat was especially tasty, salty and crusty, with a gravy dark as sin. Slowly, Robert felt a feeling of well-being begin to wash over him. It wasn't just that he was eating a good meal when hungry. It was something alleviating, something lifting from him, as if he had been encased in dross, or had been wearing an ice-shirt.

Gayla ate the way fussy women ate. She pushed around each piece of vegetable matter in her bowl, examining it before catching it with her fork, and then examining it further as she raised it toward her mouth. Eventually, she began to talk about her project and ask Robert questions. He was only half-listening because he wasn't sure really what she was getting at. Robert suspected that she chose a gritty subject because she had grown up privileged. She might as well don a badge that read "No dumb blonde here."

"So, anyway," Gayla said, with a cheerful ring to her voice. "Tell me about you."

Robert didn't like the subject, didn't like the intention behind what appeared to be an open invitation to friendship, but he wanted to talk, he found. He found, just then, that he wanted to talk.

"I'm no different from anyone elsh," he said.

"We're all different, Robert," Gayla Calley said, with a teacherly scold in her inflection.

"What you're sensing is the newness of thish, that I

am a freshman among the homelesh."

"I think it's more than that," Gayla Calley said.

Robert Walker shrugged. He was relishing the taste of the meat, which exploded with flavor at every bite.

"I have no home," Robert said. "Lotsh of us these days."

"Uh huh," Gayla said. Her conversational pause was a way to draw out other people. It was a technique.

"Itsh not too bad. Cold nights are tough."

"I bet they are."

Robert bristled again. He wasn't sure why.

"Tell me about your dishertation I am fodder for."

"Well," Gayla Calley was uncomfortable. She dabbed her mouth with her napkin.

"Go ahead," Robert said, and he couldn't help smiling. His smile relaxed his lunch date a bit.

"It's true, Robert," she said, "that I am writing about the homeless. That's true. But I don't think of the homeless as just good subjects. I mean, I don't see you as a route to a degree, if that's what you're implying."

Robert chewed some more.

"I mean, I am not having lunch with you just to further my personal ambition. I care—" She stopped herself.

"You care about those lesh fortunate than you?"

Gayla regained a little of her equanimity.

"You interest me, Robert Walker. You're an educated man, a thinking man. You have a gleam in your eye I don't see very often, especially—"

"What?'

"Especially given your circumstances. I am sensing there is a story here, a story behind the Robert of today."

"Everyone," Robert said.

"Everyone has a story. I know. Won't you tell me some of yours? Won't you trust me a little? I am sorry we got off on the wrong foot. Is it because you developed a little crush on me? You imagined perhaps a romantic spark between us? I can't apologize for that. It was not my intention to flirt with you, you know. I do think we can be friends, beyond the paper, beyond this lunch."

Robert Walker sat back and looked at Gayla Calley. She was so pretty his fortitude felt wounded. Her smile could open hearts, pocketbooks, bank accounts, closed doors, even, apparently, the path to scholastic success.

49

Robert would not tell Gayla about his life. Instead he told her anecdotes about living outside among the homeless, the drug-addled, the criminal, the gypsies and the crazed. He told her a little bit about the walking wounded, the runaways and waifs, the manic jabberers, the social predators. Many of the stories came second-hand from Whiskey Dave. Whiskey Dave had been on the streets for decades, off and on. He had stories about the legendary homeless: Dancing Jimmy, Monk Cassava, Eminence Grease. He actually worked occasionally, mostly doing odd jobs for garden shops and landscapers. Dave knew plants and he had an eye for design. He also worked once at the library as a custodian. But all of Dave's jobs were temporary by design. He only wanted to buy more alcohol and, for a time, a warm place to sleep. But, something about the outside called to Dave. It wasn't just the booze that kept him on society's fringes. It was an inability to stay part of the system. And, for a drinker, Dave was a remarkably peaceful and calm man. The whiskey took the edge off Dave and Dave stayed smooth and upright. He also took care of the less fortunate among the Outsiders. He saw this as his role.

Sometimes Dave worked at CK's on Poplar where Babyface Bill was a busboy when he wasn't on the streets. Dave thought of Bill as a little brother and together they had many adventures. When Bill was sent to Memphis Mental Health Institute for a couple weeks of drugs and shock treatments Dave held his job for

Robert Walker

him at CK's. Dave did double duty, working harder than he'd ever worked in his life. When Babyface got out, medicated and dazed, Dave stepped aside and Bill took over again, never really realizing what had happened. Bill told folks that he had been on vacation. The shock treatments left Bill slightly aphasic for a week or so but then he was back to normal, regaling customers with his tales of when he had a sheep farm in Ireland. No one could verify this but Bill's stories of his sheep farm were generally consistent.

Robert told Gayla the story about Kelly Norfleet's 3 unsuccessful suicide leaps from the bridge. He told her about Amy who only slept with the hitchhikers, the Outsiders who were only in town for a week or so. Amy's reasoning was that they were safer because they hadn't absorbed any of Memphis' poisons. She considered them clap-free, AIDs-free. Amy, who lived under one viaduct or other out near 240.

Robert told her about Jerry, with his Irish tweed cap pulled down over his bald pate. Jerry sat in the CK's on Poplar, in Midtown, talking animatedly to himself, while his wizened wife sat next to him, chain-smoking. She didn't even move when he jumped up and ran into the street, met there by a cab heading downtown. Jerry flew for a moment, a transient angel, and then he lay still, his shoes next to him on the pavement.

Robert told the story about Jimmy "Crack" Cohen who stole to get by. Most recently he specialized in the copper from business's air conditioning units. And once, when Jimmy was being booked, he dropped his pants. He thought he was at the proctologist's. And about Michelle who was so pretty she had to purposely get a venereal disease to keep the men away. Michelle started as a model and a ball girl for the Memphis Chicks baseball team. Then she got into drugs and it scrambled up her pretty head.

Robert Walker told Gayla Calley about Gwen and Terry, who used to sit outside St. Mary's Catholic Church at Market and Third, downtown, reading from The Bible and dreaming. Terry said they used to sit at the corner of the church, facing west, and imagine that the driveway was their living room. They dreamed of a home out of *Little House on the Prairie*, with weathered walls that kept them out the elements, and they would own a dog they would name Blackie. Gwen lived in an apartment once, which she said was nice and cozy, while outside it was Hell's Kitchen. The government stopped Gwen's disability checks cold and sent her spiraling down into homelessness. So she set up camp outside St. Mary's food kitchen and sang the old hymns, the ones from back and back, to the queues of the hungry.

"Gwen said," Robert Walker said, "'I have always been interested in the homeless. I didn't think I would ever become one.'"

The stories rolled out, sad, outrageous, cruel, deflating, funny and without end. Few of the stories on the street had an end. Some Outsiders got jobs, some found benefactors for a while, some found Jesus for a while. But the life on the streets went on, as inexorable as the bleeding of one year into the next.

50

GAYLA Calley turned off her tape recorder. The waitress brought cobbler and coffee.

"You won't talk about you, Robert? Not even with the recorder off?"

"For what reason?" Robert asked.

"I said, I am interested in you. You interest me."

"As a case shtudy."

Gayla was nonplussed. She wanted to get Robert to open up. She wanted to hear his story because it was important to the way her dissertation was going. She felt guilty about this and hence reticent about pushing too hard.

"It's ok, Robert. I enjoyed our lunch. I thank you for joining me."

Robert sensed something underneath the placid mollycoddling. Anger? Or self-reproach?

"I better go," Robert said.

"Where now, Robert? Can I drop you somewhere?"

"No, no thank you. I don't ride in cars."

"Ok."

Gayla paid the bill. Robert forgot the money he had in his pocket. He didn't want to pay but he didn't want to be beholden to her either. He was having a hard time parsing his own emotions.

They stepped outside and there was a shaft of bright sunshine coming from between two mountainous black clouds. The yellow sunbeam looked solid enough to walk on.

"Are you going to find Dave?" Gayla asked as they stood on the sidewalk, uncertain how to go on.

"Maybe. Dave. Pete. Shomebody."

"Pete," Gayla said, flatly.

The hair on the back of Robert's neck rose unaccountably.

"Pete the Hunchback," Robert said.

Gayla took Robert's hand. She looked at his eyes. She was seeking the glimmer there.

"Robert. You haven't heard?"

Robert swallowed hard. His eye hurt. His ear ached. The sun was like needles. He wanted to walk away. Now.

"Pete was murdered last night."

Robert went deaf. He didn't hear the rest of what Gayla said. Why was she standing there with his hand in hers and the sun lighting her perfect golden Gwyneth Paltrow hair if Pete were dead? No, it could not be true. Robert's senses shut down. He fell away from the world.

Gayla continued: "He was murdered outside the Union Mission. No one knows why. Someone cut him up pretty badly."

Gayla increased the pressure on Robert's hand. She waited for him to react. His immobility was frightening her. Robert Walker's face was a mask, white and harrowing.

51

ROBERT opened his eyes wide. He was trying to see the world again. He was trying to regain a balance. He opened his mouth wide but no sound came out. His mouth was twisted into an asymmetrical oval.

Gayla placed her face, furrowed with fear and concern, in front of Robert's but Robert could not see her. He swung his eyes round. The world was spinning and Robert was standing still. He was the axis upon which his surroundings whirled as if on some abominable merry-go-round. He could not be the vortex. He was weak, weak. He would go down. He had to move.

When Robert began running west down Union Avenue, toward downtown, Gayla called his name repeatedly. She was howling into a storm. She ran but could not keep pace with Robert's manic, all-out flight. And then a storm broke for real. The sky creased and screamed. The clouds, as black as midnight black, threw raindrops the size of quarters down upon them, as the distance between them increased and increased.

Gayla decided she could do better in her car. By the time she pulled out of the parking lot Robert was nowhere in sight. She drove slowly westward, half blinded by the storm, half blinded by anxiety for Robert. As she crossed the busy overpass at Danny Thomas and 240, her visibility was nil. She thought she saw a running figure below her on the 240 interchange. It could have been anyone. It could have been a ghost.

52

ROBERT Walker had no idea how he ended up sheltered in a 240 underpass. He was soaking wet and his clothes weighed on him as if physically pulling him to the ground. He lay face down, his hands gripping lumps of sod and mud, his fingers stiff as claws. The rain beat down around him. The traffic sounded like the bellowing of the beasts of Abaddon. Robert's head was a dwelling of wild confusion and guilt. He could not think it. He had to think it. Pete was dead. Murdered. If only he had stuck by Pete last night. If only he had followed. Who were those people he followed off into the darkness? Pete seemed so upbeat, so trusting. Was this his downfall?

Robert could not figure out how Pete went from the park downtown to the parking lot of the Union Mission and how there he could have met his end. Who were those people he went off with? Should Robert talk to the police about them? He knew nothing. He couldn't remember a single feature of them—they were so far away, and in the dark. And Robert knew that most Outsiders feared the police and never volunteered information. But Pete was so kind, so gentle. No one disliked Pete. It made no sense. And the futility of seeing reason created imps in Robert's mind. He was tired, pained, dizzy. His right eye burned. He took handfuls of wet earth and smeared them on his face and hair. He was cracked with remorse. He was crazed and, blessedly, he swooned. He fell downward toward darkness, toward impenetrable black.

Robert Walker

Robert's swoon sent him deep into unconsciousness. It was a webby, mean darkness, where visions came and went, specters and memories, half-developed and confusing. Even though he was insensate he felt as if he still had one foot in the real world, and that was dizzying and tortuous and he was battling both shadows and light.

Robert was awakened by hands touching him, hands covered in clear plastic. He was confused. He did not remember where he was or how he got there. He rolled over and there was a dark-skinned woman leaning over him. She wore a cap. Robert was sure he was still in his nightmare.

"You ok, sir?" the woman asked.

Robert tried to focus. There was a muzzy light. The rain had stopped and world looked jaundiced like an old newspaper clipping.

"Wha—" Robert said.

"Can you sit up?" the woman asked him.

"I think sho," Robert said. And with her help he rose. He now saw that she was a policewoman and that another officer, a jowly white man, stood beside a patrol car. The woman leaning over him was Latino, he thought, her skin a lovely shade of brown.

Then it came back. Pete was dead.

Robert felt the tears rising again and he didn't want to cry in front of the police officers.

"Is your name Robert Walker?" the woman now asked him.

Robert opened his eyes wide as if she had just found out his dearest secret.

"We got a call from a—" and here the officer hesitated

and looked at a pad in her hand. "Gayla Calley. Do you know a Gayla Calley?"

A sob escaped Robert's sagging mouth.

"She was concerned about you, Robert. Is there some place we can take you? She has given us her address if you want to go to her."

"N—no," Robert said. His breathing was stertorous. He covered his face with his hands and when he did so he felt the mud caked on his face and hands. He did not understand what had happened.

"Can we take you somewhere? You can't stay here," the officer said and she smiled.

Robert looked at her partner. He looked bored and clearly ready to move on from this trifling duty.

"Shaint Dymphna's," Robert said.

The officer looked confused.

"Robert, what happened to your face," she asked.

53

In the back of the patrol car Robert felt the panic welling in him like sickness. He was going to be sick. The world outside was moving too fast. He was moving too fast. And Pete was dead. Murdered. Dead.

Robert Walker lay down on the seat. The sympathetic female officer looked around to make sure he was OK.

The shame of his panic made Robert burn with a nauseating intensity. He was too hot. The air was too thick. He couldn't see yet shutting his eyes made it worse. He wanted out. He wanted to walk. He wanted to run. How far was it to St. Dymphna's?

The patrol car smelled of sweat and something else, something like old leather, or a lathered horse. The radio bleeped and blurted. The female officer was talking on a cell phone.

Finally, the car stopped and he heard the driver put it into park. He had made it. Now what? He didn't really want to go in. He didn't want to see anyone who knew him. He didn't want Erin Pound to see him like this. He began to cry again.

54

"Jesus, Robert," Erin Pound said. "What the hell?"

Robert was lying in the room where he first met Dr. D. He was filthy and he is weeping softly, with short gasps as if he could not breathe properly.

Erin was wiping his forehead with a warm, wet washcloth. Her question was rhetorical. She was not expecting Robert to answer anytime soon. Robert's eyes were squinched tight except for his palsied eye, which showed a red-white line. Erin was wiping away tears along with muck and rainwater.

Robert lay that way for a while, being ministered to, lying in half swoon, afraid of opening his eyes or his mouth, afraid that the truth that was in him would burst forth in a flood of tears and blood and pain and horror. Erin sat faithfully by. Her patience was calming. Robert Walker did not want to calm. He wanted to be engulfed by pain, by the final pain.

Robert had no idea how much time had passed. It could have been minutes or hours. The room he was in was dim, the curtains heavy, blocking out the outside world almost totally. The room was a cocoon of somnolence.

After a while Robert opened his eyes. Erin Pound smiled a soft smile. Her eyes were kind and concerned. Perhaps she was this way with everyone, Robert thought, but, for now, it was consolation.

"Ish Dr. D. here?" Robert now asked.

"No, Robert," Erin said, and her washcloth went to

his forehead again, reflexively. "Did you need to talk to her?"

"God, no, no," Robert said.

Erin smiled. "It's just us for now, Robert. I have asked a doctor to stop in later, a medical doctor. I am worried about your well-being since you came in here in such a sorry state."

Robert nodded. He didn't care. At least with a doctor he didn't have to talk.

He didn't have to talk.

This now became his fervent prayer, that he not have to talk. Yet, Erin was here. Erin, who was caring and gracious.

More silence passed. Robert closed his eyes again.

55

WHEN Robert woke he was alone. His heart began to beat frantically. What was happening? And when he figured out where he was his first thought was: who is coming for me? Have they sent for the authorities to put Robert some place...safe? No, Robert could not go someplace else. He could not.

He sat up. His clothes were clammy and soiled but someone had covered him with a blanket. Robert's head swam. He had a headache that felt bigger than his head. He thought he might faint.

He lay back and brought his knees up toward his chest. He closed his eyes and clenched his teeth. The more he struggled against the panic the more it consumed him. He felt as if he might jump out of his skin, or as if he might vomit up the revulsions of his inner life, pitchy and fetid. His chest felt thin; his blood beat too hot, too hard. Something in him screamed to get out, an alien, an afreet. He comprehended the abyss below him and he appreciated that he may tumble headlong into it. This was literal, not figurative. There really was an abyss at his feet.

And then Robert felt, like the sharp illumination of a flash bulb in an ink-black room, as if, suddenly, oh so briefly, Lucifer's Presque vu, he had seen what was behind the curtain of life and it was hideous, bleak, dangerous, vile, evil and hopeless. It was black like blindness. The door to hell cracked open. Life was hell. Hell was a split second away always.

Robert screamed.

Then Erin was back in the room. She sat next to Robert on the couch and made him sit up. She put her arms around him.

"I'm here, Robert. Do you know where you are?"

"Yesh," Robert said. It came out like a sob. He began to cry. "I can't shee," he said

"Robert, you can see. It's Erin. I am right here. I won't go away again. I am right here. Look at me, Robert. Look into my eyes."

Robert halted his vision spinning wildly round the room and brought his sight to rest on Erin's kind, brown eyes. He sobbed again. It escaped him like a beast set free.

"I was getting you dry clothes, Robert. And I was talking to Dr. Marshall. He's outside and would like to look at you when you are ready. Ok? Would you like to put these dry clothes on?"

Robert tried to stop his mind spinning loose and wild. He nodded.

"Would you like me to leave—"

"No," Robert said, more vehemently than he meant to.

"Ok, ok, here, let me pull your coat and shirts off. Ok?"

Erin Pound, after baring Robert's torso, wiped it down with a fresh warm washcloth. Robert whimpered softly.

"Can you do your pants?"

Robert shook his head.

Erin hesitated. She saw the line. She hesitated and then she stepped across it.

Erin bade Robert stand and she took his shoes and socks and pants. He stood naked before her, his head bowed in shame. His skin was peppered with goosebumps; the area around his crotch was red from soiling and inflamed patches shone like fresh sin. Erin wiped his legs and thighs with the balmy cloth. She wiped his contracted cock and between his legs and around his buttocks. Robert began to cry harder.

Once into the dry clothes, Robert lay back down.

56

AFTER this strange intimacy they were quiet for a long time. Robert lay with his eyes open. The room settled around him, the shadows in the corners seemed to brighten slightly, as if a sly luminosity were within them. Robert felt a modicum of peace descend, like a light tap to the center of his chest.

The day ticked away. Erin Pound did not move. She stayed by Robert's side and held his hand and occasionally mopped his brow.

After a long while she spoke.

"Robert, can you tell me what happened? Can you talk now? The doctor is here and he has suggested a mild calmative called Ativan. Is that something you would like?"

Robert looked into Erin's soft features and found there a true friend. Her face recalled, perhaps, images from his childhood.

"Why?" he said, and his voice cracked a bit. "Why are you sho good to me?"

Erin thought about this for a moment.

"First, Robert, it is what I do. It is my job. But, secondly, you draw me. I do feel for you in a way not strictly professional. I felt it yesterday. You seem like a man who has fallen a long way, who has fallen for a reason that might seem insurmountable to you. I see a lot of folks here and many of them are carrying burdens they need not carry. Sometimes it helps if someone tells them they need not carry such a load. Sometimes it doesn't. But, with you, Robert, I feel that you want to be free. And you don't want to disappear. You don't really want to disappear. So many people I see want to disappear, want to give up their gift of days out of despair, or desperation or just plain sadness. I don't sense that with you. Maybe I'm wrong."

Robert looked at Erin. He wanted to tell her the right thing. He wanted to be able to recognize the right thing. "I do want to dishapear," Robert said. "I do with all my heart."

And he began to weep again. But, this time, in his weeping, he found a loosening, as if a door in his core had opened. He felt, in his desolation, an anger with the world that was almost liberating. His pain opened his heart, his mind, his eyes.

57

ROBERT held Erin's hand. He could not stop the tears. He didn't try now. His palsied eye burned from being open too long. The tears did nothing to diminish its discomfort. And his ear pulsed with pain, sending shudders down his jaw.

"Robert, I don't want you to disappear," Erin Pound said.

Robert Walker hesitated one moment and then he broke open. It was a wound.

"Heesh gone," Robert said. And then a beat later, words came like sick.

"He never hurt anyone. He waz good, good, right down to this spindly little legs. He waz good, Goddamit, and he died like a bug, like an unwanted dog. Who would do it, Erin Pound? Who would stab him? Who? I don't understand. I don't. I can't shee how this could have happened."

Robert's sobs, coupled with his palsied lisp made comprehension difficult. Erin leaned closer to him.

"Who Robert? Who is dead?"

"Pete! Pete, goddammit! Pete the Hunchback. They killed him like he wash nothing. Now he'z gone, gone. I can't stand it, Erin. I can't. It's too much, too much. The degradation, the squalor, the cold, the pain, my half-face, the pain, Erin, the pain. And now heesh gone. I saw him. He wash right there with me. I let him go. He shaid he was staying with friends. And I let him go."

"How could you—"

"I didn't mean to. I should have stayed with him. I shaw the danger. I saw how things slip away from us, so easily, so shimply, Erin Pound. They fall away. Life falls away, bit by bit. I couldn't hold on. I couldn't hold on. I should have followed him. Erin, I should have done something."

"Robert, you—"

"No, I don't want forgiveness. I don't want absolution. I don't want out. I am trapped in this pain, Erin Pound. I am trapped. I should have done something. I should have held him. He was so sweet, Erin, just small, and crippled, and so tender and full of life and so shmall, so small, Erin, I couldn't hold on. They took him from me. He was so shmall. Small like the beginning of things, that small. He was little even for his age. He wash only only, Erin, only shix, and he was blond and beautiful and his eyes shown like blue ice. Oh, Erin, oh my God, my God left me. He was only only—, Goddamit, Goddamit—"

Robert curled into a ball. He brought his knees up and he let go of Erin's hand and he rocked and sobbed and his eyes were wild. He was wild. His gaze flashed around the room like lightning. And he wouldn't stop moaning and sobbing. Erin Pound was frightened. She wasn't sure what had just happened.

She reached out a hand and let it lie on Robert's shoulder.

"Robert, who are you talking about? Pete the Hunchback is dead. Yes, I get that. Who are you talking about now, Robert?"

"No no no no no—I cannot tell—ever—ever—I cannot tell. I cannot make my burden less. To tell would be a sin—I cannot do it. I cannot sin anymore. I do not deserve compassion. I cannot accept redemption. No no no. I cannot accept expiation. I have shinned, sinned, sinned. I cannot tell. I tried to save him. It waz my fault. I tried, I tried to save him. He was so small, so shmall. I held him. I tried. I didn't mean it. I couldn't help him. I held his head, his little boy's head. He wasn't even 7 years old."

Robert Walker hit himself in the face, twice, hard, with his own balled-up fist.

Erin grabbed his arms.

"Robert! Stop!" she said, vehemently. "You're frightening me."

Robert let his arms drop.

"Robert—"

"My son," Robert bawled. His face was contorted with rage and pain. His lips pulled back from his teeth. His eyes feral. His cheeks red as if slapped.

"My shon," Robert said, quieter. He was collapsing inward.

"My shon," Robert said, almost a whisper. "Nick, my son."

58

ROBERT was crying soundlessly now. He was spent. His face relaxed, the tears were gleaming on his cheeks. He felt truly drained as if his fluids were pooling around him. His limbs were tired and his chest ached.

"Robert," Erin said, softly. "Try uncoiling. Lie flat here and breathe deeply, into your stomach. You're holding your body too rigid. See if you can't stretch out and relax."

Robert moved slowly. He drew his long legs out from his body and straightened them.

"Can you talk?" Erin asked.

Robert was quiet for a long time. He was surprised to find himself still crying. He wasn't aware of the tears. Erin Pound scooted her chair closer to the couch. She set a hand against his cheek.

"You lost your son, Robert? Can you talk about it?"

"My shon," Robert said, simply. His voice was cold, mechanical.

"My Nick."

Erin kissed Robert's temple. Robert looked at her and his heart was confused and broken. His heart wanted to speak. After so long, his heart, damaged and hardened, wanted to speak.

"I," Robert said. He looked into Erin's eyes.

More time passed. Erin feared Robert was spent; his vocalizing diminished. The silence stretched out between them like a wall.

"I used to sell books for a living. University preshes.

I was a traveling salesman. It was nice work. I would drive all over the Mid-South, Tenneeshee, Arkansas, Louisiana, Oklahoma, Mish—mish—issippi."

"Where did you live then?"

Robert stopped talking. Erin thought she had miscalculated. She should remain silent. The story was coming out, however slowly, however painfully.

"I wash married. Her name was Lyn. Beautiful Lyn. Long, coppery-red hair, freckles, slim and regal. My beautiful wife, my Lyn."

There was another pause but Erin sat still, holding Robert's hand now.

"Lyn used to run Burke's Book Store. She wash the manager. I love that bookshtore. Have you been?"

Erin nodded.

"Lyn and I met when I called on the store. We had shorta known each other for years, off and on, acquaintances, shame parties, shame author readings, that sort of thing. I never thought Lyn, a woman of her clash and beauty, would go for me, but she did. She really did."

Erin smiled encouragement.

"We got married. It was a short courtship. I knew she wash the woman for me immediately. I wanted her to marry me from our firsht date on. Oh, Lyn."

Here a small sob interrupted the tale.

Robert spoke of their Midtown home, on Tutwiler Ave, a downstairs apartment with the landlord above them. The apartment was small and the heat was regulated by the landlord who lived upstairs. They were always cold in fall and winter. Robert told Erin they were happy. Lyn could cook and they ate healthy meals, lentils, veggies, hummus.

"I loved our home life. It was the first time I felt completely shatisfied in my life."

"Of course," Erin said.

"I began to hate traveling, hated to leave her for a week or two at a time. It washn't hard work but the road time killed me. I grew sad. When I wash out of town I knew a solitary deshpair. Those crappy motel rooms began to seem like prison shells, the walls closing in.

"Then Lyn got pregnant. We weren't trying but we weren't that careful either. We were very happy. We threw ourselves into it, a team effort, shuch love, caring. And we began to read everything we could find on natural childbirth, Bradley clashes, home birth. Lyn wash fierce. She was brave and so committed to thish child that I tried to follow in her wake. I tried to ride along. I wash so proud of her, and of our unborn child."

Robert faltered. He began to feel rocky as if he stood before the precipice again. He felt he had lost his place in his own story. He stopped talking and held himself stock still, like a man asleep on an eleventh story ledge. Erin recognized the rigidity of his body as a bad sign and stroked his cheek and brushed his hair away until she sensed him relaxing again. Tears still ran, slowly, a soft lachrymose susurration.

59

ROBERT told Erin about the planned homebirth that didn't come off, how Lyn did 35 hours of labor at home, heroic in her determination and stamina, but how, in the end, they had to make a midnight trip to the hospital. The hospital treated Robert and Lyn like hippies who tried that craziness called homebirth. They practically gloated over their failure. Nevertheless the baby came, a blackened, bloody alien who became instantly precious. They brought Nick home after 24 hours, against medical advice, which was duly noted on their chart.

Robert said, "He was so beautiful. Round and healthy and sheemingly happy ash a clam. We made our lives over for him. Parents do. Everything revolved around Nick, his feeding, his shitting, his shleeping or lack of it. Lyn breast-fed him with the intensity of a mother lion. It's a bond, I guess, men can't understand. Though there were fights and he and Lyn, it turned out, weren't really a good match, Robert loved being a father. He read books about how to talk to your kids; he read all of Maria Montessori's books. He held his son and walked around with him as if he were another part, a new arm, a new heart. Though the sex between Robert and Lyn dwindled, the love for the tiny newcomer overcompensated.

Traveling became doubly hard for Robert. He hated leaving Nick. And Lyn, too, of course. And when Robert came home Nick was ecstatic to see him. Later, when he learned to walk, Nick would run full tilt down the sidewalk when Robert returned to their crappy little apartment, made holy by the child's presence. Nick's joy on seeing him after a week's absence made Robert's heart hurt. Nick wiggled with the joy of being reunited. His smile, his dimples, made his father weak with delight.

As the story unfolded Robert's body rode another wave of sobs. He kept saying Jesus over and over again. Erin kept her hand on his shoulder. This opening up was like being naked, the story one of sorrow and appalling transformation. Robert was possessed by his own unspooling.

"I don't know when it started to go bad. When I returned, sometimes Lyn was distant, not dramatically so, but I could tell something was on her mind. Still, we let our lives revolve around Nick. We lived for Nick. This is not overstating it.

"I was home sometimes for a couple months at a stretch. These became difficult times with Lyn. The distance between us sheemed to grow, a widening chasm that I could not bridge. I tried talking about it. She deflected. She promised me nothing was wrong. To help make ends meet she took a job waitressing at Ronnie Grishanti's restaurant. It meant that she wouldn't come home some nights until 2 in the morning. And Nick could not shleep for long off the breast. I would put him down by 9 and he'd be up by 11. I would rock him back to sleep and he would get up two hours later again. It was very stressful. When Lyn would come in at 2 or later, smelling of smoke and alcohol, the rift between us broke into shmall spats and nasty glares. Lyn was always quick to end fights though. She could be acid-tongued but she would forget about it an hour later.

Shtill, there were many nights I went to bed alone, mad as hell and full of a new enmity toward my wife.

"Lyn thought that there is a holy order to sitting down to dinner with family. I still think of our meals that way, as rites.

"It wasn't really her fault. I can say that now. We were not well-suited to each other yet I thought she was beautiful and loving and kind. I shtill do. I still do.

"One night while she was out I was in the bathroom and a thought occurred to me and I don't know why. I thought about Lyn's diaphragm, which she kept in a drawer above the toilet. As I wash peeing, I thought about that little pink, plastic, snap-case and I tried to will myshelf not to look in it. I shook dry. I pulled my pajama bottoms back up but my eye never left the drawer. So I opened it up and found what I did not want to find. It was empty. Gone too was the tube of Gynol spermicide.

"My chest began to hurt. I thought I wash having a heart attack. I had to sit down, only to pop back up five minutes later when Nick cried out. I went to him and he had been having a nightmare. He had nightmares. Happy during the day and bedeviled at night, it often sheemed. Anyway, I comforted him by taking him back into the living room, and rocking him in my arms while watching something on Turner Classic Movies. I think it was *The Third Man*. Nick's tears ceased about the time mine began. I was trying to comfort myself as much as him. I rocked him long pasht the time he fell asleep. When Lyn came home, hours later, that was how she found us. She smiled her sweet smile at her little family pieta. And I shaid nothing to her. I could not bring myself to speak. I handed her Nick and I went to bed in Nick's room while she took him into, what we still called, our bed."

Robert Walker

60

ONE of the other workers at St. Dymphna's brought in two cups of hot tea and gave one to Robert. He had to sit up to drink it. Erin slowly stirred her cup, her face inscrutable. Robert sipped the herbal tea—it tasted of raspberry—and the heat felt pleasing on his throat. It also unsealed his ear a bit.

After a while he continued.

"A few months went by. I went out on the road again. I was blue, beaten down. Money wash tight, I wash losing Lyn and the world seemed agley to me. I could not find my sense of shelf. I was really losing my grip and being alone in cramped motel rooms was not helping. I was near panic. At night the walls of my room moved inward. Television was just another scratchy, gray wall. I couldn't eat without my stomach cramping.

"I was in Tulsa, Oklahoma, when I hit bottom. I called Lyn like I did every night. There was an eerie silence behind her. No TV burble, no music, no Nick. After a few pleasantries I asked her where Nick was. There was a hesitation, a too-careful pause. 'He's at my sister's,' Lyn said. 'He wanted to shee his cousin.' A cardiac cycle or two passed. Then a voice in the background, painfully distinct, called 'Lynnie!' A frozen silence on the phone. Lyn was clearly struggling for something to shay. I hung up.

"The rest of that trip was a blur. I cried in my motel room, a damp towel around my shoulders, the TV on low, bad show following bad movie. I didn't care. I tried to read but my concentration wash shot. Somehow I made it through and the drive home was a bleary, tired shlog. When I saw the shines for Memphis I almost kept going.

"When I pulled into our driveway on Tutwiler no one came out to greet me. I pulled my bag from the back seat and used my key to get in. Lyn was sitting in the small, crappy living room. Her hands were in her lap. She looked like a nun about to do penitence. But she was not penitent. She was in love with somebody elsh. I should have seen it coming but I hadn't. She cried. She told me she was moving out. She told me she shtill loved me and that I wash the best father and all that kind of bullshit one shays in those situations.

"I asked her what next. She told me she had already found another apartment. This seemed an especially cruel barb. This went right into my heart. She had been through with the marriage for longer than I knew. She had planned. I don't even remember what I said. Much of it washn't very nice though now, looking back, it was inevitable. We were lousy together. But, at that moment, all I knew was pain. Pain and panic and something elsh, unnamable, welling up in me like vomit. I didn't want to ask anything. I wanted her out of my sight. And I wanted to shee my son.

"What about Nick? I said, so quietly she had to ask me to repeat it. What about Nick? I said, my voice rising. 'He'll live with me,' she said. She had decided everything. She was in control. I was jetsam. Just then Nick came into the room rubbing his eyes. He had a cold and his nose and cheeks were red. His fine blond hair was tousled. Shtill, a smile broke out on his face, that smile that I counted on at the end of every trip. And it was that smile which triggered my next reaction.

"I scooped Nick up and ran to my car. Lyn screamed something behind me, I don't know what. I got Nick into the car but the car-seat was in Lyn's car. I buckled him into the front seat beside me. And I backed out fast so that Lyn could not reach the car, so that I could not hear what she was saying.

"But I did hear her scream. I heard her scream. And then I saw the truck. It was an eighteen-wheeler, much too much truck for that suburban street. Those big rigs were not supposed to be in the neighborhood but this one wash. It was like doom, large and implacable, more real than nightmare. I saw the truck. It was the last thing I saw."

Robert's head hung between his upright knees. The tea cup was upset in his lap. He was like a marionette whose strings had been cut. He was without power, without volition. He was beyond crying, beyond talk, beyond the simple ministrations one human being offers another.

"Robert, it wasn't—" Erin began.

"Don't," Robert said, and he raised his dead man's eyes.

61

THE doctor gave Robert a mild sedative, Ativan, and told him to chew it so that it would act quicker. Erin turned out the light and left him in whatever peace he could find inside his tortured sleep.

An hour later Robert woke up in the dark. He remembered where he was. He remembered that he had told Erin Pound his narrative. He didn't know whether he regretted telling her or not. It did not make him feel better. That was only in movies, he thought, that people tell their dark secret and are returned to the realm of the incarnate, returned to the walking-around world.

It was quiet in the darkened room but outside Robert could hear gabbled conversations and faintly the knocking of pots and pans. Robert always hated the murmurings behind closed doors. It reminded him of when he was a child and the adults put him to bed before he was ready to retire for the day. This room was like his bedroom, dark and close and only a thin partition away from the wailing of humankind. The walls were shifting shapes of light and dark. For the first time, Robert noticed the ticking of a clock in the room. It was an archaic sound, an old fashioned memento mori. He wondered if Erin was off work now and some stranger would come soon to roust him.

It's ok, Robert told himself. It's ok to not feel relief, clemency, tranquility. It's ok here in the dark where he could be anyone, a man lost, a man wandering, wandering evermore.

Robert Walker

62

"Robert," Erin Pound's compassionate voice came from the other side of the door. "Are you awake?"

"Yesh," Robert said, feebly. Then, rousing himself and clearing his throat, he repeated, "Yes, Erin."

Erin came in with more tea. She turned on a desk lamp which lent the room soft phosphorescence like a professorial library. She set the tea on a small teak table by the couch. The room's details began to coalesce for Robert and color and shapes and edges returned.

"You want some more tea?" she asked, sitting near him again.

"No, no thank you, Erin."

Robert's voice was roughened as if he were gargling his words.

"Are you getting hungry?"

"I am," Robert said, and he shrugged himself into an upright position.

"We're about to serve dinner. Salisbury steak and mashed potatoes."

"Elementary school food. Do you have bologna in a cup?"

Erin Pound's eyes twinkled and she laughed.

"Robert," she said. "You're gonna be alright."

"Yesh," Robert said without much conviction.

"I have a small surprise for you. I hope you don't mind. Gayla found Dave and Debra and she's brought them here to see you. They are concerned about you and would like to eat with you if that's something you might want."

Robert managed a small smile. Unexpectedly he wanted to flee.

Then, just like turning on a switch, he was very happy his friends were there. Suddenly, he wanted to see them more than anything in the world.

"Yes," Robert said. And he wiped drool from the crook of his lip and beard.

"I have cleaned your sweatshirt as best as I could. I am sorry I don't have a fresh one, or a coat. Will this be ok?" She proffered Robert's sweatshirt, a rag, yet its weight felt familiar and somehow reassuring.

"Shall we stay here for a few moments and collect ourselves before going in to eat?"

Robert appreciated the collective *we* even if it were only part of Erin's training.

"Yesh," Robert said.

63

THE light in the corridor almost made Robert stagger. It was so much brighter than the darkened den. And it was busy. Transients and staff were mixing and mumbling their way toward the cafeteria. Robert recognized many of the Outsiders but he did not speak. He was not in the mood for acquaintances.

The cafeteria area was noisy and bright. Sometimes rooms full of the homeless can seem phantasmal, like a painting by Grosz. Tonight there was a din and glare almost like a high school cafeteria. Robert Walker was temporarily staggered by the sensual overload. When his vision refocused he recognized Whiskey Dave and Debra sitting together at a small table off to the left. They had paper napkins and plastic cutlery before them. An eccentric family table setting, transitory yet benevolent. They wore expectant smiles and were watching Robert's progress through the room. Dave stood and met Robert halfway.

"Got two seats here, Doctor," Dave said and he pulled out Erin's like a courtier. Robert sat and tried to gather his wits.

"Coffee here," Dave said and handed Robert a cracked Central High School mug already sweetened and with plenty of cream. "Lemme get your meals," Dave said and bustled away.

Erin smiled at Debra and Debra lightly brushed her hair off one side of her face where it instantaneously repositioned itself.

"Hi Robert," Debra said timidly. Her food sat before her untouched. Robert knew that Debra had trouble eating in front of others.

"Robert's a bit dazed still," Erin said. "It's been a rough 24 hours."

"Yes," Debra said.

"I'm ok," Robert said without much conviction. "Terrible about Pete."

Robert's voice broke a little. He cleared his throat. Debra's lovely face turned downward, her brow wrinkled like a child's. Robert reached over and squeezed her hand fully expecting Debra to pull it away. She was usually too private for human contact. But she did not pull it away. Robert smiled his kinked smile.

"Here you are, campers," Dave said, placing two new trays of food down on the table.

"The gravy looks just right," Erin said.

Robert looked at the food and was revolted. He thought perhaps that he was about to be sick. But that only lasted a moment. Still all he could do was take a few bites of steak smeared with mashed potatoes. It did taste fine, bock dark like something which had been brewing for a long time. Robert drank some more coffee.

"Terrible about Pete," Robert now repeated.

"It is, Doctor, it is. I am trying to find out something about his death and about his body. I am not making good progress, however. I believe Pete was known at First Congo Church. Some kind of service may happen there. May be a graveside at Shelby County. I'll let you know."

"That's fine, Dave," Robert said. "We can all go together."

They ate. Some conviviality entered in. Robert began to relax. There was a murky core of sadness still present but he was lifted by the conversations, by the simple presence of these gentle people.

64

AFTER dinner Robert, Dave and Debra said goodbye to Erin. Erin enfolded Robert's hand in hers and then, as if by second thought, hugged him. Robert smiled.

It was around 6:30 and the sun was setting and the sky was rooster colored to the west and gray overhead, a soft gray like an expensive suit. The storm had passed and left an unseasonable warmth behind.

"The river?" Dave asked and pulled his ubiquitous bottle from inside his coat. He handed it to Debra first and she pursed her small umber mouth as if kissing the bottle and drank a bit. Robert let a bit of the biting alcohol into his mouth and felt it numbing his tongue and the roof of his mouth and he swallowed it slowly, almost reluctantly.

The three started their walk west toward the Mississippi where there was always life, even if only the river itself, a flow like the earth's rich blood.

"Let's go Linden," Dave said. "I always liked Linden's approach to downtown. Not quite as well perhaps as that little viaduct on Madison near the ambrosial scents of the bread factory, that, when you cross it, it feels like you are gliding downhill into the City of Delight. It's a feeling in your gut."

Debra walked beside Robert, a soft brown shadow. She was dressed the way she normally dressed, a delicate shirt covered by a vest and a sweater the color of a field mouse and about that size, buttoned only at the top, and a flowing skirt (or perhaps two) that fell from her

Robert Walker

womanly waist to the ground like a daughter of Tara. She had numerous necklaces, paste jewels and small shells on string. Her shoes, chocolate ballet slippers, were all but hidden. She seemed to be humming quietly but perhaps this was Robert's imagination.

"So, they caught Ol' Captain Queeg," Dave said. He added a little two-step as punctuation.

"Queeg?" Robert said.

"Crossed the wrong bookseller apparently. Stole from some Mississippi guy who doesn't take too kindly to Grand Theft Shoplifters. Set up a sting and arrested his sorry ass. How bout that?"

"Couldn't happen to a nicer guy," Robert said.

"The truth, Robert, the truth."

The sun was all but gone and the streetlights were beginning to glow like an oven ring heating up. There was a soft outer-space sound to the process. The three moved a little closer together on the sidewalk.

"Anyone need another swallow of the good stuff?" Dave asked, his hand going for his inner pocket.

Neither Robert nor Debra answered and Dave drew his hand back out.

"Gonna be a nice night," Dave said now. "Good sleep-outside night. Gonna be nice by the river."

65

At Pauline and Linden the trio stopped and sat on the curb. In the empurpled gloaming they resembled magi, or wandering minstrels. The area around them was a mess of blasted urban blight, a part of the city between Midtown and Downtown that had yet to see renovation. Its rubbish seemed ancient, like cracked Ozymandias.

"Ahh," Dave says. "Japanese call this 'the hour of the pearl.'"

Debra hummed a short laugh.

"Here, Doctor," Dave said, and held out his hand laughing at his unintended joke. In his fist was a full bottle of St. Joseph aspirin.

"Thanks, Dave," Robert said and shook three from the bottle. Suddenly, his ear really did hurt as if reminding him caused it. He took Dave's bottle, upended it, and enjoyed the salty tang of the aspirin mixed with the smoky whiskey. For the first time Robert noticed Dave's cap for the day. It said San Antonio Missions. The Missions, Robert thought.

They sat in peace.

Debra and Robert rested hip to hip. Robert Walker imagined he could feel her flesh, pliable and humid. He chanced a look at her face and she smiled without returning the glance.

The three watched a lanky black kid teeter toward them on a rickety bicycle. The bike tilted left and right, the boy's foot hitting the ground for stability as often as it attempted to push a pedal. In the diffuse light the figure looked like a blackened scarecrow, a burnt clown from a circus in Hell. They realized he was as drunk as a tinker.

As he got closer they recognized him as one of the young men who hung around Overton Park, normally around Rainbow Lake. His bicycle was a child's bike, at least a size too small for him and he pedaled it almost standing up.

"Say, say, say," he said. "You know Mose?"

"No Mose round here, Doctor," Whiskey Dave said.

"Mose, Mose, Mosely. You know?"

"Can't help you friend," Dave said.

Debra and Robert stood off to the side. They were content to let Dave handle things. Dave was a talker. He could talk.

"Mosely. No, Mosely. That ain't it. Allison," the fellow said. He was standing with the bike between his legs using the handle bars to steady his wobbling body.

"Mose Allison," Dave said. "The jazz guy?"

"Yes, yes, jass, jass," he said. And then once more, "Jass!"

"Ok," Whiskey Dave said.

"So you help a boy out?"

"Help you out?"

"Money, friend. Buy splilth. Whatsay?"

"You're barking up the wrong tree, Doctor. We're Outsiders, too, see. We're part of the great unwashed, free, unmonied vagabond society."

"Jus money, get me back to my wife. I need only one dollar, thirty cents."

"You're married?" Dave asked, closing one eye to get a better look at the kid.

"Got a babe, yessir," the kid said.

"You lookin' for money for your kid?"

"Yes, Mose. For Mose."

"You have a kid named Mose?"

"Thas right, Christian soldiers. Got little boy. Mose Allison and my name."

"Ok."

"Mose Allison and then my name."

"Your last name."

"Right. David."

Dave opened his eyes wide. He was smiling.

"You know me?"

"David," the kid said again as if Dave had not spoken. Mose Allison and then my name David."

"Mose Allison David."

"Thas it."

Dave laughed and turned his grin toward his friends. Debra and Robert chuckled.

Dave reached into one of his coat pockets and pulled out a well-worn single. He handed it to the kid. Dave figured the young biker couldn't be more than 18, 19.

"Thas it," he said. "Thas real, friend. Thas awful real."

He rode back the way he came. As he passed under each streetlight he came briefly back to life, a sooty angel, on a bent chariot, going in and out of the light.

66

WHISKEY Dave said, "Georges Bernanos says, 'With fearful speed the visible world seemed to slip away from me in a maze of pictures; they were not sad, but rather so full of light and dazzling beauty. How is this? Can I have loved it all so much?'"

Debra replied, quickly, without much thought, "Kobo Abe says, 'Three days a beggar, always a beggar'."

Debra looked abashed. She felt she was showing-off. "Sorry," she said.

Dave smiled as if a child of his had just graduated college.

"That's beautiful," Robert said. He took her hand. She held his and they walked that way for a while till Debra used that hand to reach up to brush her bangs back. Now the contact seemed far away, like a fancy, like a memory. Her hand was slim, her fingers tapered like a pianist's. Robert's hand felt its absence now.

There was a serene lull in the conversation. Robert wondered if he were expected to supply a quotation. The world of books was distant, back there somewhere. What was the last book he had read?

Dave and Debra looked at their friend.

"I got nothing," Robert Walker said. "Wait, I remember a joke from a Peter DeVries novel. Um, about a tramp who approaches a houshewife and holds out a button. He shays, 'Lady, could you show a shirt on this?'"

Dave smiled his piratical smile. Debra snuffled a laugh into her scarf which made Robert laugh out loud.

They walked by Southwest Tennessee Community College and there was a handsome couple hitting a tennis ball on the fenced-in courts. There was a squeegee leaning against the chain-link fence and a few damp spots still to the sides of the court. The woman was tall and brunette and her long, athletic legs made her seem ethereal, as if she didn't belong here among the sons of Adam. She glided around the court like Roger Federer. With every little flounce of her white skirt she broke hearts. Her partner, a blond fellow built like a running back, did not move as gracefully. Each step he took shook the court. He was also breathing heavily.

Robert, Dave and Debra watched them under the metal halide lights, young gods in their gladsomeness.

They walked on and the night grew darker. They were soon in an area of boarded buildings and bleak windswept pavement.

67

THE threesome passed Mount Olive CME Church and Universal Life Insurance. They crossed Danny Thomas and downtown lay before them like a mirage.

"Do you wanna walk down Beale?" Whiskey Dave asked, and once more produced his timely bottle. Debra took a small sip and so did Robert Walker. The pain in Robert's head had abated. Dave took a long swallow and replaced the bottle inside his jacket.

"I love Beale Street," Debra said.

"Pete loved Beale Street," Dave said. "Hell, Pete loved wherever he was."

"I do, too," Robert said, if only to be pleasant. But, in saying it, it rightly became so. Robert realized that he did love Beale Street, even the refurbished, whitened-up Beale, a street of mojo and ghosts. He and Lyn used to go to B. B. King's club before the baby came. Before the baby. Robert lifted his head and looked westward. Perhaps the palsied eye teared up only out of nostalgia.

"You need eye drops," Debra said, softly. Her thin, brown face looked lovely in the streetlight.

Robert smiled at her. And again squeezed her hand. They walked hand in hand for a bit.

"Eye drops," Debra repeated, almost to herself. Sometimes Debra's thoughts spiraled tightly inward and she became lost in her head. Sometimes she muttered.

Beale Street was busy but there was an almost somnolent serenity to the street. Among the neon signs and restaurants and street musicians there was a scattering of Outsiders. Dave nodded to a few who were panhandling outside Silky O'Sullivans. Beale Street was bright and clean and now stood in the shadow of FedEx Forum but there was still an undercurrent of bluesy vibe to the place, as if its history could not be extirpated. There were presences on Beale Street and their conjuring spells were made of music. In a way it was deathless.

The trio stood in front of a young black kid playing hell out of an electric guitar. His amplifier was the size of an overnight case but the sounds he was getting from his instrument were big sounds, raucous celebrations of otherness. He couldn't have been 15 years old.

Whiskey Dave smiled at the other two and Robert nodded. This is what humans do, Robert thought. After all is said and done, we can still do this.

They wandered down to the front of the Rock and Soul Museum. They peered through the glass. When they turned back toward the street there was a clan of tourists who were looking at them askance, as if they had just ruined the family vacation. Robert recognized this, too.

"Hey, hey," someone said, off to the West.

It was Bowdre and Bronwyn. Bronwyn seemed as if she had just stepped off a movie screen. She had the troubled but sweet-faced beauty of Isabel Adjani. Bowdre was still carrying his found art. It looked even worse than the day before. Some of the rods were loose and some were caked with mire now. It looked like a plant of pewter and the pewter was dying.

"Know anyone interested in art?" Bowdre said.

They had pretty much the same conversation they

had yesterday. Dave was kind and gave them a few names, people he knew worked in three-dimensional art.

After they left Dave and Robert stood smiling roguishly at each other.

"Bronwyn," Dave said.

They shook their heads. Debra smiled into her collar.

The three Outsiders walked to FedEx Forum. It was something aliens had constructed and gifted to the city. It was an enormous, outer space mushroom. The regular season was still a few weeks away but the place was lit up and seemed to glow with some kind of diabolic life. The light coming from it was wavy and viridescent and warming. They sat on the steps and watched the new life of their hometown. For better or worse the NBA had changed the city, changed downtown. Robert had no feeling either way about it but he liked the look of the edifice itself and, in his former life, he had been a basketball fan, especially of the Memphis State Tigers. At one time he had had a Keith Lee poster on his bedroom wall. What house was that? How long ago?

As they sat a small woman the color of paper and pearl approached them. She was wrapped in a layer of shawls, a quiet spectrum of grays and silvers. Her small, squinched face held some kind of mischievous emanation.

"Do you live in Memphis?" she asked.

"Yes, ma'am," Whiskey Dave said.

"I love this city," she said.

Who is this booster? Robert thought. Debra slipped her arm under his. It felt like a palliative.

"Me, too, ma'am," the garrulous Dave said. "You lived

here all your life?"

"Not yet," the old woman said and she smiled a goblin's smile.

Dave and Debra and Robert laughed.

The woman stood before them for a few moments. She looked all around her. In the neon light she might have been an aging undine.

She sighed deeply.

"Well," she said. It was what strangers said before they parted from each other. But before she left she reached into her small clasp handbag and pulled out 3 ten dollar bills. She gave one to each of them.

"Oh, now, ma'am," Dave began.

The woman held her hand up like a traffic cop.

"I've been there," she said and disappeared into the night.

68

At the river the three stood and looked across the choppy, chocolate water at the smudged lights of West Memphis, Arkansas. To their left was the old Memphis-Arkansas Bridge, rust-colored and still somehow majestic in its dinge and strength. It was redolent of the days when bums rode the rails, when they used trains as their own personal cross-country excursion conveyance. The newer bridge, to their right, formed a brightly lit M across the river. It winked off to the North, speaking of other routes, escapes, undertakings. The night had slipped away. On the river, slow like mammoth, man-made manatees, barges still worked their antiquated business. One moved before them now, as large as Noah's cruiser, but empty of its freight. Who was inside its small, weakly lit rooms? What kind of lives did they lead?

"It's late," Whiskey Dave said as if in answer to that thought.

"Yesh," Robert said. Debra's hand rested lightly on his arm.

"You want to try the shelter tonight?" Dave asked.

"It's a beautiful night to shleep outside," Robert said.

"It is," Dave said.

"Remember Red Skelton's tramp character?"

"Freddie the Freeloader," Dave said, and barked a quick laugh.

"Freddie the Freeloader," Robert Walker said.

They were all reluctant for the night to end and, for

Dave, there was still some concern for Robert's well-being.

"Tomorrow," Dave said. "I'll find out about Pete and we'll make some plans. You wanna meet at Java Cabana in the morning. Mid-morning, I mean?"

"Yesh," Robert said.

"Could be that gorgeous black singer you like will be there."

"Valerie."

"Right."

"Good to see her, eh? Good for what ails you."

"Yesh."

"You going back to the park?"

"I think so," Robert said. Really, he didn't know. He wanted to stay with Debra. He also felt so tired that he thought he might be running a fever.

"What about you, Love?" Dave said to Debra.

She ducked her head. She was smiling a wee smile. She looked up into Robert's face. She found there some level of ardor.

"I think I'll make sure Robert is ok," she whispered.

"Just so," Whiskey Dave said. And he kissed her on the cheek.

He and Robert hugged and Dave made his way North, toward Mud Island and the radiant but empty Pyramid.

"To be continued," Dave called back.

They watched him walk away, a hitch in his step, but still with that compact ball-player's carriage.

"Winter coming soon," Debra said into the air.

"Yesh."

Debra and Robert started the long walk back to Overton Park. Once they reconnected with Union Avenue it seemed an easier stroll straight East, a long, aching, undeviating thoroughfare from the river to Midtown. Union was busy. There were many restaurants and bars still open. They passed The Memphis Convention and Visitors Bureau, The Cotton Museum, Main Street, where they had to wait for a late night trolley trundling by, holding only two passengers, an old woman in the rear and at the furthest extreme from her at the car's front a correspondingly old man. Perhaps they are a couple, Robert Walker thought. Or perhaps they will be by night's end. Robert and Debra passed November 6th Street and the Peabody Hotel, still majestic in yellow-gold trim and sulfuric brilliance. Across the street was the alley where The Rendezvous was, where they crafted the best ribs in Christendom. They passed AutoZone Park where the Memphis Redbirds played, New York Suit Exchange, the offices of the city's daily paper, The Commercial Appeal. It was animated like a hive, open all night. And at Marshal, Sun Studios, where Memphis became Memphis. The Scottish Rite Masonic Lodge, University of Tennessee Medical Center, Methodist University Hospital. And then, at Watkins, the Cupboard, still shimmering with captured illumination. Robert felt a twinge of nauseated shame but they continued walking, moving, against the night's unreliable mettle. The traffic was moderately heavy. Someone yelled something from a car as they passed but neither Robert nor Debra heard. They held hands more firmly now. Their grip on each other was stauncher.

69

Iт had cleared and the night sky was the tint of unpolished silver. There were a few bruise-colored clouds. The moon seemed as close as a face, a hand, another body.

The streetlights made warbling phantoms in the places where water still pooled on the asphalt. The streets shone like pyrite.

"I wrote a poem about you, Robert," Debra said, softly.

The way Debra said his name stopped Robert's heart.

"A poem?"

"Yes. A little poem."

"I didn't know you write."

"I started at Door of Hope. Do you know Door of Hope, Robert? They have a writer's club."

"I've heard of them. I don't write."

"You could, though."

There was a rutilant flush to Debra's cheeks.

She added, "I'll show it to you tomorrow."

"Tomorrow," Robert Walker said.

And then Debra went quiet. For her it was an astonishing flow of words and Robert Walker was grateful. He felt nimbler, almost pain-free.

A new freedom, barely felt, unknowledgeable, surrounded them like a nimbus.

70

THEY entered the park, off Poplar, at the entrance to the zoo and the College of Art. There were still some lights on in that direction. Perhaps there were some young artists there sketching late into the night. Perhaps there were lovers developing photographs in the dark room, kissing as pictures of street people developed in mystic trays of fluid.

As they crossed the golf course Robert remembered the gay lovers. He remembered the rotting pig. Was it only yesterday morning? Robert walked cautiously down the path and repositioned a protective arm around Debra. He detected no bad smell. Someone had taken the pig away.

When they got to Robert's spot, his little declivity between two trees, surrounded by kudzu, Robert saw that there were new blankets, an army blanket and a used comforter, within his boxes. And a new shower curtain for rainy nights. He saw the hand of Whiskey Dave in such largesse. Robert said a quick prayer that wherever Dave was that night that he was safe and happy and slightly inebriated.

The blankets felt good though the ground was unforgiving. Debra ducked down and was beside Robert Walker before he had time to think. Her clothes were damp and he put his arms around her and under her shirt her soft, brown skin was warm like blood. She snuggled against him the way a child would. She rested her comely face against his shoulder. Robert's heart ached. He gently ran his hands down the gentle slope of her back. She smelled good, like the earth after rain, like vanilla and woodsmoke, and something deeper, loam, black soil, a thing chthonic and sustaining.

Robert felt something foreign against his chest. It was the paperback of *All the Little Live Things* that Mary had given him in Java Cabana. He pulled it from his sweatshirt pocket and lay it down near their heads.

Robert nuzzled Debra's neck and put his lips against her cheek. He licked her skin softly and she tasted of salt. Robert pulled his blanket around her.

Debra slipped off her clothes hastily. She unhooked her voluminous skirts and slipped out of them deftly, with a ballerina's grace. Robert took his off, too, with measured slowness, while simultaneously trying to keep her close. Soon her body was against his. It was a small miracle, an end-of-the-day benefaction. Debra kept her face averted. Robert wrapped them both in the fresh blankets.

"Robert," she said. Her voice was wee. It was like the breath of the surrounding forest.

Robert Walker's penis was erect against Debra's smooth stomach. He put his arms around her, tenderly. He felt her warm russet skin, ran his calloused hands over her ribs both soft and hard at the same time. He stroked her round bottom.

"Robert," she said again, a sigh.

"Sh—" Robert said.

"I'm sorry," Debra whispered back.

"Sweet Debra, I was shaying" Robert said.

"Oh."

"Debra."

"Don't—do—this," she said into Robert's chest, a murmur.

Robert pulled back deliberately. He made himself still.

"You want me to stop?"

Debra looked at Robert with her dark roast eyes. She repeated, "I. Don't. Do this."

"Oh, yesh, I see," Robert said. "Yes, Debra." And he pulled her close again.

Debra put her hand around Robert's penis. Robert believed he was in dreamland. Neither moved for a long time. Her grip was loose, as if the breeze encircled his cock. Then Robert realized Debra had fallen asleep, naked, against his chest. Her soft palm still held his penis, which remained semi-erect.

Robert then joined her and they both slept like Adam and Eve, after the fall.

Robert Walker did not dream.

fin

Special thanks to Cheryl Mesler, Rebecca Tickle, Ashley Harper, David Tankersley, Steve Stern, Steven Millhauser, Richard Bausch, and Amanda Bausch, for encouraging words along the way.

COREY MESLER has published in numerous journals and anthologies. He has published 8 novels, 4 full length poetry collections, and 3 books of short stories. He has also published a dozen chapbooks of both poetry and prose. He has been nominated for the Pushcart Prize numerous times, and two of his poems were chosen for Garrison Keillor's Writer's Almanac. His fiction has received praise from John Grisham, Robert Olen Butler, Lee Smith, Frederick Barthelme, Greil Marcus, among others. With his wife, he runs Burke's Book Store in Memphis TN. He can be found at www. coreymesler.wordpress.com.

www.ingramcontent.com/pod-product-compliance
Lightning Source LLC
Chambersburg PA
CBHW020838260626
47169CB00003B/1040